Requisite Release

By Charles Georgiou

From April 2022 until September 2022 a 23-year-old male by the name of Simon was referred to our clinic. Simon had been recently diagnosed with depression and a course of Cognitive Behavioural Therapy was recommended by his General Practitioner. Whilst under our care it was discovered that Simon suffered from severe anxiety as well as an existential obsessive-compulsive disorder. Through CBT we attempted to treat Simon's depression with an active focus on the creation and discovery of meaning in his life.

We have compiled all the doctor's notes, session notes and Simon's journal for analysis and evaluation.

For the sake of anonymity certain names and addresses have been redacted from the text.

North West London Clinic
[redacted]
London
[redacted]

Date: 31st March 2022

Greater London Mental Health and Wellness Centre
[redacted]
London
[redacted]

Subject: Referral for Cognitive Behavioural Therapy

To whom it may concern

I am referring my patient Simon **[redacted]** for Cognitive Behavioural Therapy.

I have been Simon's primary care physician for the past 15 years. Based on the last two appointments I believe this to be a necessary course of treatment.

Simon visited me a little over a month ago to look into sudden weight loss, fatigue and lack of motivation. I conducted a series of tests and all results showed no physical problems. I decided to speak to Simon on a personal level. After a lengthy discussion Simon opened up about some of his thoughts and feelings. The cause for concern came from certain phrases and expressions Simon had used; he mentioned that he felt "hopeless", "no longer saw any reason for his existence" and was "struggling to carry on". This has led me to believe that Simon's lethargy and fatigue is stemming from a possible mental health issue.

I strongly believe Simon is suffering from mild to moderate depression and I would like to see if a course of Cognitive Behavioural Therapy will help his condition.

I am initially recommending a 10 session course. Please contact me directly for any further information or any questions you have.

Kind Regards

Dr Edmund **[redacted]**
Tel: **[redacted]**
Email: **[redacted]**

Greater London Mental Health and Wellness Centre
Cognitive Behavioural Therapy Assessment Form

Name: Simon **[redacted]**

Date of Birth: **[redacted]**/1998

NHS No: **[redacted]**

GP Name and Address:
Dr Edmund **[redacted]**,
North West London Clinic,
[redacted], London, **[redacted]**

Please explain in your own words the problems affecting you?

I no longer have any motivation to live my life. I have no energy, or passion. I am always low and I am always drained. I do not know why I should carry on.

Are there any situations or events that trigger the problem or make it more severe?

The thought of doing anything, seeing anybody, waking up and just living a normal life, making normal everyday decisions. I cannot do this anymore. I feel disappointed at my inability to function, especially when I compare myself to how I used to be. But I cannot bring myself to live any more. My spark is gone.

Are there any situations or events that help the problem or make it easier to manage?

When I am asleep.

How often do you experience this problem?

When I am awake.

How is this affecting your day to day life?

I do nothing. I try to sleep as much as I can, the more I am sleeping the less time I have to confront the truth. When I am awake it is constantly staring at me, following me, surrounding me, spreading across my entire existence. It is in the essence of everything and in the face of everyone.

How is this affecting your relationships?

They have been destroyed.

Do you ever have thoughts of self-harm or suicide?

Yes.

Are you on any medication?

No.

Do you take any recreational drugs?

No.

Have you ever had therapy before? If yes, please give details on what this was for and how you feel it went.

No.

27th April 2022

Patient: Simon **[redacted]**

Session Number 1

Today was the first session with Simon **[redacted]** and this was one of the most challenging sessions I have experienced as a therapist. Simon was referred to us by his GP to undergo a CBT course due to signs of depression. Upon reading Simon's assessment form I too saw clear signs of moderate depression and a personal crisis.

Simon came into the room with an emotionless expression on this face. His long dark hair was untidy, his face carried a light unkempt patchy beard. His eyes were very dark and his skin extremely pale. He looked drowsy. Based on what he mentioned in his assessment form I would wager that these were symptoms of oversleeping. He was wearing a creased grey t-shirt with grey jeans. The t-shirt had a large stain right in the middle, possibly a food or a drink stain. His left trouser leg was tucked into his sock. He was wearing black loafers, they looked old, worn and tired.

I stood up to greet Simon but he immediately took a seat. I got the impression he wanted to get started, not because he was eager to begin but because he was eager to finish. I introduced myself and began discussing CBT and what it offers. I noticed that throughout the entire session Simon was unable to look me in eye, he constantly stared at the floor. The emotionless expression on his face did not change, not once, the same persistent expression. Simon has already decided this is to be a futile exercise.

In the initial conversation with Simon I found out surface level information. 23 year old male who lives at home with his mother. His mother works full time for a commercial cleaning company. His father passed away from cancer, Simon was 18 months old at the time so he has no memory or experiences of him. No siblings or cousins.

Simon studied English Literature at the University of **[redacted]** but dropped out in his 3rd year. Other than saying "there was no point" he did not elaborate as to why he dropped out.

Upon leaving University Simon eventually found a job as a barista for a coffee shop in the city. During the 2020 epidemic Simon was made redundant and has not tried to find a job since.

This was all the information I managed to get in this session. I would initially say that Simon displays very low levels of extraversion, particularly around the friendliness and assertiveness facet. Simon was very quiet throughout the session, he didn't have a lot to say and when he was talking he was looking at the floor the entire time. I tried to move the conversation on to more serious matters but Simon refused to engage. I asked Simon to open up about what was bothering him, to explain his problems and what he wanted to achieve from CBT. Simon however dismissed my questions; instead he insisted that there was "nothing worth talking about", he told me that this was all a waste of time, that the idea of attending CBT was an overreaction from his mother, and he no longer needs any help.

I pulled up his assessment form on my tablet and started going through some of his answers. I asked about his lack of motivation and energy and if this is still a problem. I assured him that if it is still a problem CBT can help, we just need to work together. Simon did not respond. I then brought up the "truth" that he has "confronted" as this was something that really intrigued me in his assessment form. I asked if he could elaborate on this, and explain a little more what this meant. At this point Simon just turned away, his lifeless expression stared out the window. From then on he refused to participate, he would not respond to me, he had completely disconnected from the session, he was gone.

I failed to make any progress on the crucial points I needed to address. The session ended and I felt very disappointed. Simon is clearly suffering from depression and is in need of urgent help but we made absolutely no headway today. I fear that without any effort on his behalf we are just wasting time.

The homework for next session is for Simon to come ready to discuss his thoughts and feelings. I have asked him to spend the week thinking about what is truly bothering him and how he would like to improve. Furthermore I have asked him to build up the motivation to attend the next session prepared to discuss this at length.

4th May 2022

Patient: Simon **[redacted]**

Session Number 2

I spent the whole week thinking about how this session would go, the failure of last week stuck in my mind and I was thinking about it near enough every day. I was expecting Simon not to turn up so I was quite happy when I saw him arrive, in fact it felt like a victory. Unfortunately that was the only positive of the session.

Simon entered carrying the same emotionless expression as before. He was wearing the exact same clothes, the loafers, the grey jeans with the creased grey t-shirt, the same stain sitting in the middle. His hair was still very messy, his beard just as dishevelled, his eyes were dark and puffy and his skin even more pale. As soon as he sat down he stared at the floor, his foot was shaking, he felt agitated, once again he could not look me in the eyes. I could tell he wanted the session to be over as soon as possible. His mother most likely forced him to attend this session again. This is what I find very disappointing, I cannot help someone who does not want to be helped.

I started with a mood check, Simon just said he was "the same as always". When I asked him to elaborate he didn't respond. I asked if anything significant had happened since the last session; he just shook his head. I then asked about the week's homework. I knew the answer before he could say anything. Still staring at the floor, Simon quietly mumbled, "What homework?"

I actually felt frustrated, for the first time, I have never felt frustrated with a patient before. There have been patients who have failed to complete their homework, this is common, but to forget, or pretend to forget that the homework was set, this has never happened before. I didn't want Simon to see my frustration, I am certain that if he sees my disappointment I will never see him again and I am not quite ready to give up on him.

I quickly moved the session along, I wanted to get some more information out of him, something, anything at this stage. I just feel that the more comfortable he gets in talking to me the more he will share. I asked how his mother was, and how it has been with her this week. He admitted that his mother has high hopes for these sessions and "she cares too much". I am not sure what he meant by that statement, I tried to probe but unfortunately that was as much as he would say about his mother.

We moved on to more trivial things, I wanted to lighten the mood. I asked about his taste in music, films, video games but to each I got the same response, "I have no interest". I responded asking why he has no interest. Simon refused to answer any more, he turned his head, the lifeless expression once again staring out the window, pretending I did not exist. At this point I had to be honest with him. I told him that CBT is pointless unless you work at it, I explained that he needed to be honest as to why he is here and what he wants to change. I said that I needed his cooperation, he will not improve unless he tries, and if he is not willing to try there are plenty of people who are suffering that are willing to try; his presence in that seat is denying me the opportunity to help someone else. He did not respond, he did not react; he carried on staring out the window pretending that nothing was happening.

It occurred to me that the most information I have got from Simon was the initial assessment form. This was emailed to him and he filled it out in the privacy of his own home. He has said more in that assessment form than he has in the past two sessions. He is after all a student of literature, perhaps he is better at writing down how he feels.

Based on this idea Simon's next homework task is to start a weekly journal. I have asked him to write down his thoughts and feelings throughout the week; what is bothering him and causing him distress, any significant events or even just random thoughts. I would like him to write this down and to email this to me the evening before our session. I am hoping I can open Simon up more this way, if he is more comfortable in writing I can at least read his thoughts and attempt to help him. I do not know if this will work, but it is worth a try. I did however make it clear to Simon that if he fails at the homework again we will have to terminate the sessions. To this I got no response, not even an acknowledgement, nothing.

Before he left I reminded him that even if his mother is forcing him to attend, he has made the effort and found the energy to attend. Deep down, he wants help and I am here to help him.

From: Simon@**[redacted]**
Sent: 10/05/2022 - 23:49
To: Linda@**[redacted]**
Subject: Simon's Journal

I do not want to live a life of mediocrity.

11th May 2021

Patient: Simon **[redacted]**

Session Number 3

I am pleased to say that Simon did open up a little more in this session. We are definitely not where I was hoping to be by the end of our third session, but I have managed to get a bit more insight into Simon's problems and I feel I'm in a better position to help him.

I was not expecting Simon to complete the journal and I was surprised to have received his email late last night. It was a very short log, however the fact that Simon thought about something and actually wrote it down and emailed it to me shows me that there is still a part of him that wants help and wants to try.

Simon arrived wearing the same clothes as the past two weeks. The stain still remained on his t-shirt. The drained and tired look was still stuck to his face, however his facial expression was somewhat different, instead of the previous emotionless expression, Simon looked slightly sombre this time round. The eyes that I had previously seen as lifeless now had a hint of sadness. He sat down, he stared at the floor and held his head.

The mood check revealed nothing, and there was no significant event that took place since last session so I pulled up Simon's email on my tablet and recited his sentence "I do not want to live a life of mediocrity". Simon did not react, he carried on staring at the floor not saying a word. I pleaded with him to elaborate on what this meant and finally he began to open up…

Simon had always seen himself as special, his mother would often tell him he was a special child, a great human being, put on the earth for great things. Simon truly believed this and would often remind himself of this fact. He didn't know what he was meant to do, all he knew was that he was "destined for greatness" and he was waiting for life to "deliver him to his calling", to "fulfil his purpose". Simon believed there was a fundamental and important reason for his existence, there was a reason that he was here, "in this body, on this planet at this time". He has been waiting his whole life for his life to make sense.

After explaining this to me he went quiet. He still refused to look up at me but I could see the tears welling in his eyes. I asked if he still believes he is special, he shook his head. Simon admitted that he is finding it painful to accept that he is not special, that he never was special and there was no supreme purpose for his life after all.

"If I died tomorrow there may be 2 people who would genuinely care. If I died tomorrow what would I leave behind. What is my legacy? I wouldn't even be remembered. Eventually I will be forgotten and it would be like I never even existed... If I was meant for greatness I would have realised something by now, but there's nothing."

Simon is trying to come to terms with the fact that he is "just an average human living a life of mediocrity". Simon explained, the belief that he was a special individual has kept him going all these years. Whenever he was in dark place, in a difficult time he would always tell himself that there was a glorious destiny he was fulfilling. This belief has functioned like a crutch he has leaned on, especially at his weakest points, it has been able to keep him going. This has now been pulled from under him and as expected he is struggling to carry on.

I asked him when he started to realise this, he said he started to feel this way around the second year of university. I asked if this was the reason for his low mood and lethargy, he responded – "only part of it". I asked if this was "the truth" he had previously mentioned, he responded - "only part of it". I asked if he could please explain what the rest of "the truth" is, at this point Simon completely shut down. He stopped talking, turned his head, the lifeless expression returned as he now stared out the window. This was as much as Simon would expose in this session. I tried to find out more information about his idea of greatness and what his idea of mediocrity is but he would no longer respond. I didn't want to push too much, I was pleased with the amount he had opened up anyway.

I am seeing traits of narcissism in Simon's personality and I believe Simon's depression is clearly stemming from the idea that he is not living up to an entitled and exaggerated sense of self-worth. Simon's use of the phrase "destined for greatness" reveals hints of a messiah complex. The fact that Simon is falling short of his own idea of superiority and greatness, has led him to develop a core belief that his life is of little importance and as such, of little value. Common with a core belief of this kind is a feeling of failure, a lack of motivation, enthusiasm and disinterest in the world around including personal relationships. Oversleeping can become a side effect with such emotions too.

In order to start seeing an improvement I need to get Simon to understand - just because he is not living up to his personal idea of greatness he is still worthwhile and a valuable human being. But, there is more Simon wants to say to me that he is not letting himself and it is crucial I know if we are to advance any further.

Simon opening up in this session was down to the journal, he managed to get his feelings out, even if it was a short note this helped immensely in our discussion. As homework I have asked Simon to continue the weekly journal, although this time I have asked him to explain "the truth" to me as best as he can. I told him that I need to know the full picture if I am to have any chance in helping him. Encouragingly, Simon nodded at the homework task, showing me he understood and was prepared to try.

From: Simon@**[redacted]**
Sent: 17/05/2022 - 19:37
To: Linda@**[redacted]**
Subject: Simon's Journal

Can you care for something that does not care for you? Would you carry on or would you stop? This is what I am struggling with.

I was once the main character, my book had been written, my path was set. It seems the truth possessed the power to burn all my pages in front of my eyes and scatter the ashes right into the chaos, leaving me there, alone.

I have never been a religious person, but I always felt as though I was in the presence of something bigger. You could call this a deity but I would describe it as the universe itself. After all I am conscious, I am part of the universe and how can a part be more complex than the whole. The universe is everywhere, it is everything. It sets the rules, creates the matter and starts the motion. And I am a product of its creation, I am here and I always felt as though it was watching over me, following me through my journey to fulfil the reason for my existence, the reason it brought me here, out of the void and into reality.

As a teenager I would often stare up into the sky and speak to the universe. I never got a reply, there must be a reason I thought. When I felt rejected – there must be a reason, when I failed an exam – there must be a reason, when I was bullied – there must be a reason, when I was lonely crying in my bedroom, when I was scared, angry, worried, guilty – there must be a reason. Just be patient – there is a reason.

My childhood wasn't the best, I suppose it wasn't the worst either. I never knew my father, all I had was my mother and all she had was me. My mother would often fill my head with delusions of grandeur, telling me I was important, special, I was here for a purpose, the universe had big plans for my life. I believed it all and I was proud. She would also tell me wonderful stories about my father, how he was strong, powerful, intelligent, loving and caring. I believed it all and I was proud. I don't think any of it was true. My father was just a mediocre man, lately I doubt if he existed at all.

You keep on asking me to explain the truth to you. But once you learn it there is no going back. If you want to know I will tell you, but you must face the consequences, this is *your* choice.

The truth hit me when I was in my second year of university. Life was ok at the time, I had a group of friends, there were five of us, we met in halls and we were sharing a house together. They were a fun bunch but only in small doses, too much time with them and I would start to get stressed. They would often moan that I didn't go out with them enough, or that I spent too much time in my room. I thought I gave them enough of my attention, sometimes too much. I was also a year into a relationship with Joanne, a girl I met at the student union one evening, she was a quiet girl, didn't really like doing much or saying much, I think that's what I liked about her, we could just stay in all day and all night, hardly say a word to each other and she would be fine with it, she didn't expect or want anything more. I don't think I had strong feelings for her, it was just convenient. Studies were going ok, I wouldn't say I was the best student but I was doing ok, to be honest I liked the material I was studying but I was always accused of being lazy, I on the other hand always felt I gave as much effort as I was meant to. Nonetheless, this was probably the best period of my life. The peak before the fall, I guess ignorance is bliss.

We were coming to the end of the second year, it was a Wednesday morning and I had a meeting with my course tutor, Professor Albert **[redacted]**. On the way to the meeting I stopped to grab a coffee. I was in the que, in front of me was a mother with her child. The child must have been around 4 or 5. After the woman ordered she moved to one side to wait for her drink. Her child remained in front of me. She turned to her child and said "come over here darling, let the man order his coffee". I smiled and thanked her. I grabbed my coffee and an apple and made my way to the campus. I took a sip of the coffee and a bite of my apple, just

22

then something lodged itself into my mind that I couldn't shake. "Let the man order his coffee". The man! Was I a man? When did I become a man? I didn't feel like a man. What is a man supposed to feel like? What makes a man a man, is it just down to age or is there more to the essence of being a full grown man. This stayed with me. I could hear her saying this over and over. I thought about it for the entire walk to the campus and right to Professor **[redacted]** office. The truth was calling me. It was faint, and it was distant, but it had begun.

The meeting with Professor **[redacted]** started as expected. We discussed the year gone and the year ahead. What modules I was doing well in, what modules I needed improving in and ideas for the final dissertation. He then reminded me of the fact that I was going into my third year, the final year. He asked the question that woke me up, the question that jolted my ignorant mind to discover that I was now at the start of another journey. "What do you plan to do after you have finished your studies?" What did I plan to do? Why had I not questioned this before? Every part of my life so far I was a passenger in a car. I was being taken on a journey and this whole time I was waiting to be delivered to my destination. But, now I was being told that I would soon have to get into the driving seat in order to carry on, there was just one huge problem, I had no idea where I was going. What next? The faint call was getting bolder.

Why had I not asked myself this question? I tried to think - what did I think my life would look like. When I was a child, a teenager, last year, last week - how did I picture my life? What did I want to do? What did I want to be? Where was this destination I believed I was heading to? I couldn't answer. I have had fantasies about the great and glorious Simon. The books they would write about me, the documentaries they would make, the statues they would build. Streets, parks, charities, all named after me. I would be immortalized, I would be admired, celebrated and loved. A true hero, part of the fabric and the history of the universe, fulfilling my great purpose. But what was I great for? What is my reason for being here? I always thought this would be decided for me, in fact, I believed it *had* been decided for me. I thought I was here for a reason and I was following my path. I thought my calling would come to me, it would make itself clear to me and I would just know when I am meant to know, when the universe wants me to know. But now I was wondering - where is the greatness I was promised? Where is this purpose I was destined for? Where is the meaning I have been waiting for? I was asking and as always I received no reply.

Weeks later I was having a lazy Sunday afternoon with Joanne. We got to talking and eventually the conversation moved onto our studies. Joanne asked me what I planned to write my dissertation on. I told her that I didn't know, she responded "well you have to decide". Like a dagger across my face, those five devastating words scarred me beyond recognition. Right then I realised something significant, something I had never admitted to myself before – I am free. There is no book, there is no destiny, no determined fate. I am free to decide. I must decide, I must act; it is all down to me and me alone. My life is in my hands, and there is nothing else to it. The universe has no great purpose for me, the universe is not guiding my path. Simon is a tiny man in an infinite universe that cannot reply. I am like everyone else, I am part of the herd. Just a collection of cells that has no significance. Walking thinking matter that doesn't matter; I am mediocre.

This is all I could think about for months, I agonised over this, the more I thought about it the more painful it became. I was falling deeper and deeper into this despair and finally I hit the bottom. And there it was. The naked unadulterated truth. Beware. It is not that my life lacks a great and supreme purpose, it is that *life* itself lacks all purpose, life itself lacks all meaning. The universe never responds because it cannot respond. It has no rationale, it has no intention. It – just - is. We are not created, we are just a random collection of particles that has appeared in the chaos. We appear and in a blink we are gone and it doesn't even matter. All we have is a short slice of time in an empty universe devoid of purpose.

We are not here for a reason, nothing is here for a reason. There is no objective meaning. There is no grand narrative.

The search was over, I had finally found the truth and there was nothing there. This is it, and this is all it will ever be. There is nothing more to life.

After I discovered this I deteriorated, there is no point to anything and so no point in doing anything. How can I be expected to carry on if I have nowhere I am supposed to be? My friends would ask me "what's wrong". Nothing, that's actually it, nothing is wrong, nothing is right. What use is morality, strength, courage, loyalty? What use is friendship or love, they all mean nothing. These are just words masquerading as big strong ideas, but like a house of cards, they stand tall and powerful until you touch them, then they fall apart, revealing the emptiness that they are hiding.

Everything around me lost its value. Life lost its value, so I stopped trying. The idea of doing anything seemed tedious and pointless. I gave up on everything and everyone. I dropped out of university, I stopped going out, I stopped seeing Joanne and eventually I just left the house. I didn't even say goodbye to the boys, there was no point. They mean nothing to me, I mean nothing to them. I moved back home, in my old bedroom with my mother down the hall. I tried to work for a bit, something to occupy my mind for a few hours a week, but even that didn't work out. Right now I have nothing. I guess almost nothing. I'm still holding on to the value of meaning. I can't drop it, and because I can't drop it everything has lost its essence and this is what hurts the most. Nothing matters. Life is empty, just me, alone, gripping the value of meaning so tight my fingers are bleeding. I wish I never saw life as it really is, I wish I never discovered the truth. But here I am, wondering why I should carry on, wondering why I should continue to exist in a dead unconscious universe that does not think feel or recognise my existence. The universe cannot care, so why should I?

Freedom offers infinite options with no reason to choose. I am paralysed by indecision and indifference. Sleep is the only thing left, I choose not to choose. I do not want to play this game anymore. There is no point to it.

18th May 2022

Patient: Simon **[redacted]**

Session Number 4

This was a very productive session with Simon and I now feel I understand exactly what he is going through, putting me in a much better position to help him.

I read his weekly journal last night, as soon as I received it. This revealed a lot and I finally understand his idea of "the truth". Simon's depression is stemming from a complete loss of meaning, he seems to be suffering from existential rumination and it is now developing into an obsession. Simon has developed a core belief that there is no inherent value in existence and life. By carrying this core belief Simon has stopped trying to live as he sees no compelling reason for his life and life in general. This best explains the lack of motivation and enthusiasm that Simon has previously described. Based on this email I would say Simon displays very high levels of neuroticism, I also see he leans to the lower levels in conscientiousness and the higher levels in openness to experience, especially around the imagination and intellect facets. I believe the combination of these traits in addition to high introversion explains Simon's over thinking, negative emotions, and struggle to improve. However now I understood the full extent of the problem and with more of an insight into his personality I was ready to try and work on a solution.

Simon came into the room still wearing the same loafers, grey t-shirt and grey jeans. There were more stains on the t-shirt this time. It appears that he has not showered in a while. His hair was still very untidy and visibly greasy. Simon sat on the chair and stared at the floor. There was a timid look on his face, as though he was embarrassed with how much information he divulged in his email.

I asked how he was and how his week had been, as usual I didn't get much information. I congratulated him on completing the homework task and I was very impressed with the level of detail he expressed. He didn't react. The priority was to get Simon talking again, I needed to open him up. I decided to ask him a question point blank, something that will get him thinking and hopefully talking - "What do you mean by objective meaning?" He instantly looked up, bewildered and intrigued by the question. For the first time Simon looked at me straight in the eyes. I tried not to react, I wanted to keep him calm. He stared at me in silence, I repeated the question and I told him to take his time. Eventually Simon answered in an almost dubious tone. Simon claimed that objective meaning was an intentional design that had been created by something bigger, "a numinous truth that makes sense of our existence." He explained that with no supreme narrative, "the story doesn't matter". Simon carried on and I let him speak, uninterrupted, I needed him to open up as much as possible.

"I can choose to move or remain idle, either way it doesn't matter. And so there is nothing that pulls me out of bed anymore, there is nothing that is telling me to get up and move. That voice that was there has gone, and it has left nothing behind".

Eventually he stopped, he buried his head into his hands and quietly asked "can I be helped?" I asked Simon what he wants, ultimately, what does he want to achieve from these sessions.

"I want to feel, something, anything but emptiness. Can I be helped?"

I assured him that he could, but that he needed to work with me and I needed him to try. He looked up at me again and nodded.

We carried on discussing the concept of objective meaning. I asked Simon an important question that he strongly needed to consider - "why is subjective meaning less valuable than objective meaning?" He leaned back in the chair and began thinking. He inhaled, he went to speak then paused. He started thinking again. Eventually he responded – "because subjective meaning is not real". I asked him to consider what he meant by real – "Something that is external to the individual, something that remains true outside of someone's experience and existence."

I then asked if his pain was any less real as it did not exist outside of his experience. I asked if my current thoughts were not real because I was the only one who could experience them. I explained - "they live in me, and they will die with me, are they not real?" Simon was silent.

I asked what his opinions of the world would have been if he never existed. He replied that this was a stupid question - "I would not exist to have an opinion". This was precisely my point; life only exists because we are here to perceive it. Truth, meaning, value, purpose - they can only exist if the individual is there to experience them. These concepts live and die with the individual, they cannot be objective because they are fundamentally subjective by their very nature.

"You have to exist first, then you have to perceive them in order for them to exist. How can there be truth if there is no one to perceive it? How can there be meaning if there is no one to experience it? You have to create them or else they cannot exist, they do not exist outside of your perception. Their existence is our perception."

As I was explaining this Simon remained still, focused, his attention was locked. I felt he was genuinely interested in what I was saying. He may not fully accept this right now but I am beginning to challenge his core belief and this is vital. When I finished speaking, there was a moment of silence. Eventually Simon asked –

"How can I create meaning in a meaningless world?"

I was honest with Simon about the situation at hand and what lied ahead of us. His depression stems from being unable to answer this significant question and as a result it has turned into a constant and repetitive thought, always on his mind and consuming his cognition. This is very much pointing to what is referred to as Existential Obsessive Compulsive Disorder, and he will not be able to continue living until he finds some sort of satisfactory answer that he can live with. This is a tough task, it can only be answered bit by bit, but we can get there, we have already started. The first thing is to focus on cognitive distortions, I need Simon to start changing his thought process and get that single negative thought [life is meaningless] out of his head. Once we change the beliefs the actions will follow. If I can stop him believing that life is meaningless we can start building some meaning into his world. If he holds on to this belief it will not be possible.

I laid out the ABC's of CBT and explained what is involved in an Activating event, leading to a Belief and then a Consequence. For homework I want Simon to make a note of any activating event that leads to the negative belief. At this point I have asked Simon to repeat the phrase "the meaning belongs in me, I create the meaning". If we can intervene at B hopefully we will start seeing an improvement at C. I have asked Simon to document this and email it to me before our next session. He acknowledged the assignment and said it was something he would try.

I started telling myself that the meaning was in me, I really did. But by the end of the week I stopped. The truth will not let me go, not yet. I can feel its claws in me, as I am typing this they're digging deeper than ever.

Thursday morning I woke up, as with most of my mornings I just lay there, staring at the ceiling. Usually I would stay there for hours, sometimes all day, I would only get up to use the bathroom or maybe get some food. The same question comes into my mind the instant I wake up – why should I bother today? I never have an answer, so I stay there. But this time I saw this as the activating event, I told myself "the meaning belongs in me". This time I had an answer – to create meaning. I got up.

My mother was happy to see me up for breakfast, we had a brief conversation and then she went to work. I sat at the kitchen table trying to think of what to do. Do I watch TV, what should I watch? Listen to music, what music? Clean my room, go out for a walk, go out for some coffee, go to the cinema, what film? Read a book, what book? So many choices, what do I choose, what do I do? My heart started beating fast, I started sweating, I couldn't think, I couldn't make a decision, not like this. So I sat there, I just sat there, for the rest of the day, I couldn't decide.

Friday morning I woke up, I stared at the ceiling and asked myself why I should get up today. To create meaning. I got up and the infinite choices laid themselves in front of my mind. Again I was paralyzed, my mind was telling me "if I can do anything I am not meant to do anything". I saw this as the activating event, I reminded myself that the meaning belongs in me, but I will not create any meaning sitting in my room considering every possibility. I needed to move, I needed to act. That crippling feeling started creeping in. Pick something, pick anything, just make a decision! Coffee! I will go out and get a coffee. So I did. I was relieved.

I went to the closest coffee shop and ordered the first coffee on the menu, I didn't even bother considering the options. As the barista was making it I noticed a coin collection jar on the counter. It was a collection for a child protection charity. It was almost full. There was no one else in the coffee shop, the barista had her back to me. I thought about taking it, actually, I thought about why I shouldn't take it. What reason was there for me not to take this jar of coins? Because I could be punished? But if I desired the money, and I was in a position where I could take the jar without being noticed, what is actually stopping me from taking it. Because it would be immoral?

But morality has no truth, it has no value, it doesn't mean anything. So why shouldn't I take the money? I grabbed the jar and I started thinking, I could put this jar into my bag and there is nothing to stop me. I could steal from a children's charity and it wouldn't mean anything. I then saw this as an activating event, and suddenly it all made sense. If I create the meaning then I can create morality. If I create morality then I would rather live in a world with less suffering children, I don't know why but that is what I would prefer. My actions need to reflect this. I wouldn't want my actions to add to the suffering of children, no matter how small these actions may be. It doesn't matter if the opposite opinion is no more or less valid than my own, this is my moral code, if my actions shape the world I live in then I want to shape it to a world I would prefer to live in. I put the jar back. The barista came with my coffee, I paid her with cash, she handed me my change, I put it in the jar and left.

Saturday morning my mother asked me if I would like to accompany her to the supermarket. I didn't want to but I didn't want to stay in bed all day either, this way at least the next few hours were decided and I didn't have to agonise over what to do. She was pleased that I was coming.

We arrived at the supermarket, it's been a while since I've been I forgot how big it was. An endless stack of aisles, an infinite amount of products displayed, hundreds of people walking up and down, trolleys crashing into each other, overfull baskets on the floors, ques for the cashier, ques for the self-checkout, staff running up and down, customers talking, staff stacking shelves, announcements on the intercom. It was chaos. I followed my mother, she followed her list, as I was walking through I could feel everyone looking at me, they knew that something was wrong with me, they could tell the battle I was going through in my head, how I didn't fit in, how I was a broken person. I knew they were all whispering to each other about me, judging me, laughing at me, it was horrible. I tried to ignore it, I thought I would concentrate on helping my mother and getting out as soon as possible. As we made our way round the supermarket I suddenly felt as though I was being swallowed up by the perpetual products surrounding me. There were 5 different types of tomato sauces to choose from, 10 different types of shampoo, 50 different types of crisps, 100 different types of chocolates. I couldn't believe the choices. I looked around and people were grabbing their items, putting them in their trolleys and moving on. Grabbing an item putting it in the trolley and moving on. Everyone knew what they wanted and they grabbed it, except me. Am I the only one who doesn't know how to find order in the chaos? Am I the only one who is struggling with freedom? How can I find what I want in life when I am constantly surrounded by endless options? Each one as meaningless as the last. I suddenly found myself struggling to breathe, I began to tremble, my vision started blurring. Something was not right, the chaos was devouring me; I had to get out. I told my mother I needed some fresh air and I ran out of the supermarket, I could not leave that place quick enough, as I was running for the door I was unsure I would make it out alive.

When we got home I helped my mother unpack the shopping. She made us a cup of tea and we sat at the kitchen table. She was on her laptop scrolling through a florist website, she said it was her sister's birthday coming up and she wanted to send her some flowers. She then turned the lap top to me and asked me what I thought of a particular bouquet. I ignored her. She asked me again and I shrugged, she asked me again and then I just snapped at her... "it doesn't matter, they're just going to die, they are going die and get thrown away so who the hell cares. Stop asking me because it doesn't matter!" I didn't even think about saying this, it just came out, but there it was again, the inescapable truth. We are all going to die, sooner or later we are all going to be thrown away and ultimately nothing will matter. Every decision I make, every thought I have, every act I do, it will not matter. I will be gone and the universe will carry on oblivious and apathetic, so why should I bother trying. Why am I delaying the inevitable? What's the point? This was the activating event that beat me. I haven't left the house since.

I've been think about death a lot since Saturday. When I was younger I used to fantasize about my funeral all the time. I'd imagine hundreds of people all crowded at the burial, they'd be crying their eyes out, all of them saddened by the loss of such a great person. As they're lowering my coffin into the ground the sky would start roaring, loud thunder booming in everyone's ears. The sky would then open up, lightening would crash down onto my coffin, bolt after bolt after bolt. As everyone is panicking and screaming in confusion I would burst out of the coffin and fly up into the sky. I would be glistening in electricity, and I would emerge, reborn, powerful and true. Everyone would bow to me, I would be the one who peaked into the other side and came back to bring the logos, to set humanity right, and there it is, my purpose, my great destiny. I don't think about this anymore, now when I think of death all I can think of is the final end, the abyss that awaits us all – nothingness; that is the only truth. I suppose it's not really that bad, I don't really understand why we all fear death so much; all of us, we try to avoid it as much as possible. From the moment we exist our cells are coded to self-destruct, we are meant to die, it's the only thing we are meant to do, yet we always try to run away from it. There's 90 year olds still getting medication and undergoing surgery just so they can squeeze a few more pointless years into their existence. But why? It's not like they will hold on to their memories, it's not like they will live on, they will decay along with their body and everything they have ever seen, felt or done will die with them, so what's the point? When we die there are no regrets, there are no ambitions, wishes, pride, shame, there's nothing. We try to avoid death but perhaps life is the unnatural thing, we have an innate disposition to run from what is real and instead we try to find that which does not exist. Life is a cruel prank. We are just walking talking thinking contradictions. But with death there is peace, no ambiguity and no chaos, just- nothing. So why do we fear death so much? I guess people spend their whole lives trying to avoid the unknown, but really they are spending their lives trying to avoid the only certainty.

25th May 2022

Patient: Simon **[redacted]**

Session Number 5

Simon's recent journal log revealed quite a bit more information. It seems when confronted with a lot of choice Simon suffers from anxiety and mild panic attacks. He explained this happening on two, almost three occasions last week - when considering how he was to spend his day, and the incident at the supermarket. Simon has alluded to this inability previously, although he has mentioned this as seeing no reason to choose. I believe months of refusing to make any sort of decision has damaged his ability to decide and now that he wants to try and start making decisions he is debilitated and feels suffocated by the choices. The fight or flight response seemed to have been triggered at the supermarket, I believe this to be linked to the confrontation of too many options and possibly a "chaotic" environment. The inability to make a choice is most likely down to over analysing each option, an expected side effect of existential rumination in combination with high neuroticism. In addition to this Simon will see no compelling reason to choose one option over the other. There may also be a lack of confidence in himself therefore questioning if he has the ability to make the best decision. This was an important point I needed to raise in the coming session.

Other than analysis paralysis, the recent journal log highlighted a high self-conscious facet and showed hints of suicidal thoughts towards the end. There was a lot of talk around death, and the idea that it can free one from pain. This is very concerning and definitely needs addressing. Simon's core belief is leading him to a very dark place so I needed to reinforce the positive thinking this session and hope he carries it for the rest of the week.

On a more positive note the log did in fact show that Simon has been trying and is following through with the homework. The beginning of the week seemed promising, and although he fell towards the end Simon initially seemed enthused to find and create his own meaning. The event at the coffee shop showed that positive thinking can yield positive actions. If we can consistently reinforce the idea that he has the power to create a meaningful life we can hopefully silence the core belief that life is meaningless and start seeing better behaviour. The beginning of the week showed this was possible.

Simon attended the session this morning still wearing the same black loafers, grey jeans and unwashed grey t-shirt. Again he looked very drowsy and very untidy. He sat down looking disappointed, as though he had failed me, he was staring at the floor, he was struggling to look at me again. Although this was upsetting to see it did in fact show me that he actually cares. This is a huge improvement compared to where we were 4 weeks ago.

I started with the mood check and he said he was feeling very low today, he explained that after the events last week he doesn't think there is any hope, that life has become unbearable. I congratulated him on attempting the homework, I reassured him that he will not be successful in every homework assignment but the important thing is that he always tries. He was still staring at the floor but he was listening, he nodded. I asked him what he felt went wrong with the previous homework task. Still looking at the floor he began describing the anxiety he felt when faced with any decision and how troubling this is for him.

"How can I expect to live my life with an inability to choose? How can I create meaning and purpose when I can't even choose what to do with my afternoon?"

I asked Simon how he got here today. He said he got the bus. I asked him if he was forced to come, "did someone grab you, drag you down and place you on the seat?" He shook his head. "You got up, you took the bus and attended the session, was this not a choice?" Simon nodded. I also reminded him that in the recent journal he described how he decided to go and get a coffee, he decided not to steal the money, he decided to go shopping with his mother, and of course last night he decided to write down his thoughts and feelings and email them to me.

"These are all decisions that you have made, choices you have selected. You can either focus on the times you couldn't decide and replicate that behaviour, or you can focus the times you did decide and replicate that behaviour. The power is always in you, whether you move or stay still, whether you do or do not, you are in control, you steer the ship."

Simon slowly lifted his head and made eye contact. He didn't say anything, he was just thinking, there were a few moments of silence. Eventually Simon asked how he could control the feeling of dread he gets when having to decide. He was referring to the anxiety and panic attacks he suffered. He said that he felt powerless, "I was at the mercy of every negative emotion I have ever had." I discussed breathing exercises with Simon that have proven successful with other patients suffering anxiety and panic attacks. When he feels the anxiety building he needs to just stop, close his eyes and block everything out, silence every voice outside and inside, take a deep breath in and exhale, repeat 5 times whilst constantly telling himself, "the dread is in me and I can stop it. The power is in my mind and I can control it. I am in control, I am in control, I am in control." Simon agreed to try.

"Always remember, the dread is coming from inside, it is not an outside force. It is created by you and can be destroyed by you".

"I am in control" Simon said. I smiled and nodded in approval.

I moved the conversation on to the birthday flower scenario with his mother. I asked Simon if he has been having suicidal thoughts; Simon confessed that he has.

"Sometimes it feels like the only thing that makes sense. If something doesn't have a purpose or a function then we discard it. Life doesn't have purpose so why do I hold on to it. I don't have an answer anymore. I try to sleep as much as I can, I guess I can make that permanent, I won't need to worry about waking and carrying on this sham."

I asked Simon if he has ever watched a movie, read a book or listened to a song. "Of course". I asked why he bothered starting if he knew it would eventually finish. "To enjoy the experience."

"Exactly" I said. "It doesn't matter that it will come to an end, all things come to an end, it is about the experience in the meantime, nothing else matters. Yes, we all will die one day, we don't know how and we don't know when, so all we can do is make the most of the time we have. If nothing you do will matter when you die, then make sure it matters when you are alive. You need to enhance your experience. All we have is the here and now. There's an eternity of death, but a short time to live, please do not waste it."

Simon's eyes grew wider, I could feel my words actually made sense to him. He thought about what I said and eventually responded – "but I don't know where to start." I explained that this is what we need to work on, and we will.

The homework for next session is for Simon to really think about what he wants from his life and make a list of things he believes will add value and meaning into his world. Based on this list we will address and work on each, one at a time. Firstly, I am hoping Simon will really analyse his life and rediscover what he enjoys, what will bring more joy to his world, something to bring back his motivation and ultimately something that will give his life more meaning. If he can visualise this he can perhaps recall a sense of happiness or satisfaction, and hopefully divert his obsessive thoughts of existence to a more pleasant place. From there we can put together a plan to start working on each point with the goal of creating a more valuable experience. Secondly, I am hoping this will help with his indecisiveness. If Simon can see himself making a major life choice, then perhaps other everyday decisions will seem uncomplicated and easy.

As I have now discovered that Simon's depression is also met with anxiety I will be recommending for Simon to begin a course of SSRI. I believe this will help with both issues, and in combination with the therapy sessions I will hope for a bigger improvement.

Greater London Mental Health and Wellness Centre
[redacted]
London
[redacted]

Date: 26th May 2022

North West London Clinic
[redacted]
London
[redacted]

Subject: Medication Recommendation – Simon
[redacted]

Dear Dr **[redacted]**

I have been Simon **[redacted]** clinical therapist for the past 5 weeks through his Cognitive Behavioural Therapy course. Our sessions and discussions have confirmed that Simon is suffering from moderate depression as well as anxiety both linked to a development of existential obsessive compulsive disorder.

I have no doubt that CBT is helping Simon and while a lot of progress has been made since Simon first visited me I strongly believe he would benefit from starting a course of Selective Serotonin Reuptake Inhibitors. The medication in combination with therapy will be the best approach in helping Simon at this stage.

Based on my recommendation I am writing to you to prescribe Simon with the relevant medication. Should you have any questions, or if you would like a copy of the progress reports, please contact me directly.

Kind Regards

Linda **[redacted]**
Clinical Therapist

Tel: **[redacted]**
Email: **[redacted]**
Mob: **[redacted]**

From: Simon@**[redacted]**
Sent: 30/05/2022 - 23:53
To: Linda@**[redacted]**
Subject: Simon's Journal

Everybody wants to get to heaven. It doesn't matter if you are religious or not, we all do. Religious people think if they act in the right way they will find heaven in the afterlife, whereas non-religious people think if they act in the right way they will find heaven in life. Ultimately it's the same thing. This is what this exercise is isn't it Linda? I can list all the great and wonderful things in life, and if I act right I can achieve them all and find heaven. I have been thinking about my personal heaven all week and all I am reminded of is the biblical story of the Tower of Babel. Human beings united to build a tower that would reach heaven. God got angry at this attempt and as punishment he confounded their language so they could not communicate with each other and then scattered them across the planet. I haven't stopped pondering this; why did God do that? I thought the God of the bible wanted people to reach heaven, why then would he have thwarted an attempt to find it? It is obvious, isn't it? Heaven doesn't exist, God was trying to shield the people from finding out the truth. Heaven is a lie, heaven on earth, heaven in the afterlife, all of it, it doesn't exist. We can build and build and build, try and try and try, but we will find nothing, there is nothing there. Speech was confounded so people could not understand each other - is that not what we have now? Each person, with their own meaning that means nothing to anyone else. We are alone, no one can understand us and we spend our time searching for something that does not exist.

Still, I don't want to give up before I have tried, let me at least starting building my own tower of Babel. As you said, life is just about the experience, if I find value in building the tower then maybe just building the tower is all I need.

What can give my life more value, what can give my life more meaning? The main thing I have always wanted was respect and admiration. This is what I always thought was waiting for me. To be seen as great, special and important. This, I truly believe will add the most value to my life. To wake up and know what I am meant to do, to know that what I am doing is a vital part of human existence. To know exactly what my role is, my one and only role and the glory that comes with it. But, and as we have discussed before, I am not great, no matter how much I deserve to be. I have achieved nothing and I don't think there is anything on the horizon. I am still mediocre, I need to start managing my expectations and being realistic about who I am. I need to find what can give an insipid life meaning.

The first thing I thought of was money, to be rich, to have a lot of wealth and material possessions. Am I being unrealistic again? I suppose most people would want to have vast amounts of wealth and there is a reason for it, money can buy pleasure, money makes you a more admirable person, a more attractive person. You're never short of friendship or romance when you're rich. You're never short of anything. Cars, houses, holidays, the best food, the finest clothes and the most magnificent jewellery. To be part of the elite, to have whatever you want whenever you want. This sounds fantastic but my expectations are running wild again. Let's be honest, as much as I may be great at being rich, getting rich - that's another story. It's not like I will be inheriting that kind of wealth, I will have to make it! Firstly, it is highly unlikely that I could even figure out how to make such huge sums of money, but even if by some miracle I did, that's not even the hard part, no, the hard part is actually doing it, working hours and hours and hours. Days, weeks, years doing nothing but working, devoting my whole life to making this money. By the time I get to the stage of having enough money for the extravagant lifestyle I will be old, tired and all I will probably want is a couch, a TV, a blanket and a takeaway pizza - exactly what I have now. So what is the point of working all those years? Life is about the experience, right? Why waste my life working excessively for money I cannot enjoy. This seems pointless, so I guess money will not make the list. Well not entirely, we all need some money to live, I still need food and shelter and I need a way to pay for these things. I cannot live off my mother forever. Maybe if I can just get a regular job, earning a modest salary, a typical role for a mediocre man that will allow me to fade into irrelevance with the rest of the herd. I will waste some of my life working but not of most it. I will have less possessions but at least I will have more time to enjoy them, and what I do have will feel even more special, that's the balance. Besides, what does vast amounts of money offer apart from a life of hedonism, there must be more to life than being a slave to your sensory desires? Having everything you want all the time will eventually desensitize you. Nothing will be enough, nothing will satiate, just constantly chasing the next pleasure. No, I think less is more, a simple job will suffice. So there we go, first point, a job, I would like to find a job and start working again. This could add more value to my experience.

Then my mind went to love. Lately I have been feeling lonely, I have really felt the need to have someone loving by my side. I could find a partner, get married and we could live the rest of our lives together. Every day waking up to a woman who loves me unconditionally, loves me for me, she looks after me, appreciates me, she cherishes all my quirks and idiosyncrasies. She loves spending time with me and I love spending time with her. We can go for walks in the park hand in hand. We can have candle lit dinners. We can look into each other's eyes with a burning passion knowing deep in our hearts that we complete each other, we bring out the best in each other, we belong to each other, we need each other, our souls are bound, intertwined, not by fate but by choice. In a world of pain and detachment we found elation and devotion, and we will hold onto it till the end. We found true love. This sounds magical. But am I idolising love? What is the reality? We are infatuated with each other at first, then we marry, soon the conversation runs dry, we have nothing new to talk about, nothing interesting to say. The quirks and idiosyncrasies that were once adorable now become insufferable. The arguing starts, days and weeks of ignoring one another. We are bored of each other, every day waking up to the same face, every night closing your eyes to the same face. We start to age, the attraction fades, soon I start lusting for other women and she starts lusting for other men. By the end we cannot stand the sight of each other and we regret the wasted years we have spent. We ruined each other's experience and we hate each other for it. We divorce only to realise we are too old and set in our ways to find someone new. We die, bitter and lonely. I guess you cannot know which way it will go. Do you risk the pain of dying love for the bliss of enduring love? Or do you remain alone, protecting yourself from the pain whilst depriving yourself of the bliss. I suppose I could take a gamble, true love would add more value to my experience. So there is the second point, to find a partner and fall in love.

Family? Everyone seems to think family is the most important thing. I struggle with this. I grew up with a very small family so I do not have much experience here. No father, no siblings, no cousins. Pretty much just me and my mother. Lately I have resented my mother, I blame her for not preparing me for real life. She kept me in a bubble, in a state of ignorance, she hid me from the truth. I know she done it out of some kind of love, to protect me, to keep me away from pain. But she should have known that eventually I would find the truth and that I would enter the real world. Instead of conditioning my mind over the years to be able to absorb the pain of reality I was sent out naked and weak amidst the chaos. I took a huge unexpected whack right in the face and I haven't been able to get back up since. No love or affection can make up for this. I question if it is worth having a family of my own, to create another contradiction, a poor mind awakens looking for an answer that isn't there. On the other hand, creating a life, guiding it through the world, preparing it for the harsh reality, this would give me responsibility, it could give me purpose, it could add more value to *my* existence. Is this selfish? Could my child grow up resenting me, cursing me for bringing them into this world? Possibly. This may have to be one I discuss with my future partner.

Friendship? I suppose this is an area with some foundations as I already have friends, although I haven't seen or spoken to them in a while. We all met at university and we did have some great times. Colin is probably my best friend, he is quite a benign easy-going person, meagre in looks but very kind, always happy to listen and always tries to please. Thomas was the leader of the pack, typical alpha male, tall, handsome, with a strong deep voice that oozes confidence and dominance. But like most dominant people everything was a competition. He liked to boast about himself and to mock others, quite a spiteful character actually, he would sometimes call me a weirdo or a loser if I didn't want to go out drinking. But damn was he funny, always the life and soul of the party, everyone wanted to be close to him. Then there was Andrew, a very intelligent person, he was studying physics I think, worked day and night, very regimented, first one up and the last one to bed. He was top of the class and had to stay there. He would always moan at me for leaving the kitchen in a mess, all the dishes had to be done right away, I didn't understand it, I would tell him that I'd do them eventually, I didn't see the big deal if they sat out for a few hours. Every week he would clean the bathroom, the only one in the house who would do it, we laughed at him because we knew we never had to clean, even if he insisted someone else should clean he would eventually end up doing it. Then there was Antonio, he was studying graphic design. I liked talking to

Antonio, we would often talk about things like theology or philosophy, we both loved sci-fi movies and we would always discuss them. He would also be the one to arrange the evenings out, he would somehow find new clubs or bars to go to, and he would always try to bring me out. So that was the group, but the question I have is - were these people true friends, or just convenient acquaintances? Was this just a group of people I would occasionally get drunk with and laugh with but deep down we all knew there was nothing more to the relationship, no true friendship. What do I even mean by true friendship? Loyalty, honesty, people I can rely on when I am struggling, people who will laugh with me at my best and carry me at my worst. How can you ever know if you have friends like that until it's too late? People these days are so fake it's hard to trust anyone. You should see the stuff I see on social media, every single moron posting snippets of their days trying to portray the perfect life. It makes me sick. I wish there were truth filters for personal photos, the type you get on news articles that vet how reliable a story is. So when some idiot posts a loving picture of him and his girlfriend there can be a disclaimer saying "she cheated on him two weeks ago, they argue every week and he's secretly been messaging her best friend". Or when some vain imbecile posts a half-naked picture of their abs and chest the disclaimer can state "he works on his body as he has confidence issues and low self-esteem". That would be perfect, either we can expose all the fakes in our lives, or people will stop incessantly posting every useless part of their existence. Do they honestly think anyone actually cares about their meaningless lives? No one cares, they know it yet they all lie to themselves to chase likes and comments, thinking it will fill the emptiness inside. All it does is expand the void and turns you into caricature of yourself. The fakeness in people makes it impossible to build any genuine relationships. Personally I think most people deep down want to see others suffer, very few are actually happy with other's success. Just like Thomas they see their relationships as competitions, it's a zero sum game. Someone else's success is your loss as they are some way or somehow beating you. If you are doing better than them they curse you for it, if you aren't doing as well they laugh at you, or worse still they pity you! Should I surround myself around people who secretly want me to fail? Is a laugh over a pint worth a silent malediction? I don't know, laughter and joy can enhance my experience. Who knows maybe there will be some genuine loyal people who actually care about my wellbeing, I think Colin could very well be. So yes, friendship will be on the list.

This is all I can think of right now. I have no idea if these will help me create any value or meaning in my life. I have no idea if any of these will add to a better experience or if they will just deliver a mediocre life, dull and plain, like everyone else; a meaningless lemming following the herd, going through the motions until death comes to rescue me. Something is still screaming at me that this is a futile attempt to create something that doesn't exist. Maybe, maybe not. There's no harm in trying. Let's start building the Tower of Babel, if it collapses I will be no lower than I am now.

1st June 2022

Patient: Simon **[redacted]**

Session Number 6

Simon's latest journal log was very interesting to read. He did complete the homework task I set and listed all possible things he could work towards in order to improve his life. As I had hoped, Simon showed progress in making decisions, he exercised the ability to make big choices with regards to the direction of his life. What was interesting was seeing the duality in Simon's thought process, he was acknowledging the value of each point on his list whilst simultaneously denigrating and dismissing them as worthless. The discrepancy in his thought process shows me there is still part of him fighting every single step of the way. The existential rumination is still giving a loud voice to the negative beliefs, and because Simon displays such high neuroticism these negative thoughts are present in all areas of his life and they are not quietening down. In order for Simon to be fully committed on improving his situation there needs to be a strong focus on silencing the negative voices whilst promoting the positive side. I need to get Simon to visualize himself achieving every goal and living his best possible life. If he can imagine a better more fulfilled life this will hopefully energise him to try his best with minimal doubts.

Simon arrived still wearing the same stained grey t-shirt, grey jeans and tattered loafers. He took a seat and stared at the floor. He still looked tired, drained and fed up. I conducted a mood check and Simon just said he was feeling the same, "not worse but never better." There were no significant events that took place this week that he wanted to discuss with me. I asked about his sleeping patterns and if he was still oversleeping and finding it difficult to get up. He nodded in agreement. "It's still the only thing I can bear."

I then asked Simon about the medication and if he had picked up a prescription from his GP. He confirmed that he had and that he's started taking the tablets. I stressed how important it was for him to take the prescribed amount every day without fail, that he should take no more or no less, and that he has to stick to it. Simon said he understood. I also mentioned that he doesn't need to be embarrassed about taking this, it has been prescribed to help. At this point Simon rested his hands on his temples. I asked if he was ok, to which he replied..."I thought you were supposed to help me, does it just make your job easier to put me on drugs?" I was a little taken back by his response, I had to reassure him that I am here to help him, that the medication is meant to work in parallel with therapy, and together we can expect the best results. "Will it honestly make me feel better or are you just trying to cripple my mind?" Again this response stunned me. I made it clear to Simon that the drugs have proven to help with one's mood and energy, and this in effect will help with improving his thoughts, behaviour and life in general. Simon nodded, "I understand, I suppose there's nothing to lose." Again, I am seeing the negative thoughts and pessimism infect all areas in his life, even the idea of taking prescribed medication that's meant to help.

I pulled up the latest journal log on my tablet. I congratulated Simon on successfully completing the homework task. I told him how impressed I was that he sat down and really thought about what he wanted in life, made a number of decisions and compiled them into a list. Simon shrugged his shoulders. I then mentioned that the entire list was muddled with pessimism and defeatist thoughts...

"You seem to have described the very best parts and the very worst parts on all aspects of the list. Do you think that if you try you will end up with the worst or that you will end up with the best?"

Simon shrugged again. "I don't know."

"Are you afraid that if you try you will end up with the worst, and this is holding you back from trying?"

"I don't know."

"Shall I tell you what I think?" Simon nodded, I continued... "There are two Simon's living inside you, two opposite Simon's fighting to get out, fighting to take over. This polarity, this constant battle is causing the distress, it's causing the indecisiveness, and it's causing your dread."

Simon instantly looked up at me and stared me dead in the eyes. There was a few moments of silence. "Do you agree?" He slowly, almost suspiciously, nodded.

"Your latest email to me was a perfect example of this. One Simon sees the magic and beauty in love, the other Simon ridiculed the idea and dismissed it as ultimately failing and leaving you miserable. One Simon saw the value in friendship whilst the other Simon had the worst opinion of all people and wants to pull away. One Simon believes starting a family is something special and meaningful whereas the other Simon sees procreation as selfish and complicit in the suffering of another human being."

Simon's eyes were locked onto mine, he was nodding the entire time. He was hearing something he knew he felt but hadn't heard in words before.

"The last couple of years, the negative Simon has been in full control, he has been controlling the thoughts, controlling the behaviour, while the more positive Simon has been suppressed and pushed out of the way. To be honest I didn't even know positive Simon existed until 2 weeks ago. But he is trying to come out, he is speaking more, he was all over that last journal you sent me. Both Simon's were, they were both fighting for the keyboard trying to make themselves heard, trying to take over."

"I don't know which Simon is the real me."

"They both are".

I then went on to explain that while he is drowning in questions about the nature of his existence, one Simon sees no meaning or value in life and sees no point in trying or making any sort of decision. Whereas the other Simon wants to create meaning and value in life and wants to start choosing, but unfortunately he can't because the other Simon is holding him back. However, although he may feel powerless, ultimately both Simon's are him, he controls them both and he chooses which Simon is in the driving seat.

"Remember what I told you to repeat... The power is in me"

Simon repeated it in unison. I smiled. I then asked, "where do you see yourself in 10 years if you only listened to positive Simon?"

He paused, leaned back and began to think.

"I guess in my own house, living with a girlfriend or wife. Surrounded by friends. Independent and forging an experience that will make me happy."

I was very pleased with this answer. He could see this type of life for himself. But then as expected he the rumination continued...

"But this is just a mediocre and pointless existence. There will always be a part of me that's screaming, that's telling me I am lying to myself, that I am valuing the meaningless, that I am living a lie. Anything I grow to love or care about will eventually be ripped away from me and it will not even matter, nothing I care about matters, I'll be trying for no reason, I'll be fighting a losing battle, I'll be..."

I opened my eyes wide, gesturing to Simon to take note of what had just happened. This was the negative Simon trying to come out again. He realised and stopped speaking. He dropped his head into his hands and stayed there, eventually asking...

"How do I silence the negative Simon?"

"This voice will not go away without a fight. You will see or feel something you believe will add value to your experience and then you will hear a voice trying to diminish its value, it's at this point you know that negative Simon is trying to take over. You need to remember that you control him, the power is in you. Push that voice to one side and remind yourself that positive Simon is trying to create a brighter better life, trying to create meaning and find value. You are the architect of your existence and you are here to build, not to destroy."

Simon was nodding with an inspired look on his face. He agreed with everything I said, he acknowledged that in the last few weeks he could feel the two Simon's battling for control, and he promised he will try to silence the negative side.

We moved on to the homework for the coming week. My plan is for us to start working on his list, to start building and creating that better experience, but not just yet. There's some work around Simon's decision making I need him to address and at the same time I need him to control the darker more pessimistic thoughts. Once I can see some progress here I will feel comfortable to start working on the list. This being the case, the homework for next session is for Simon to make a different decision every day. This does not included deciding not to decide, Simon must act every day, he must choose to do something that he enjoys every day and each evening he must update his journal and email this to me. I believe Simon will struggle, but during the struggle Simon can practise getting his darker side under control, and if he succeeds it will demonstrate improved decision-making abilities.

Simon agreed to the homework in an almost eager tone. This will be an important week to see how we can proceed with CBT.

I spent the first half of the day cursing you. You are the one forcing me to do something, forcing me to choose. I woke up this morning knowing I had to do something otherwise I would be letting you down, the more I thought about it the more I wanted to just stay in bed - the more I wanted to stay in bed the more upset I got about letting you down - the more upset I got the more I wanted to stay in bed and so on and so on. My mind was burning. I didn't know what to do or where to go but I knew I couldn't stay lying in my bed. Nowhere to go and nowhere to stay. The hours were going, it was close to 2pm and I still hadn't moved. I felt the anxiety building inside me. I was so furious that you were putting me through this. Is it really me choosing if you are forcing me to choose? Every second I spent on my bed I could feel the air being sucked out of my body, but still I couldn't move.

I remembered the breathing exercises you told me. I closed my eyes, I reminded myself that the dread is in me, I am creating it and I can stop it. I have the power. I was taking deep breaths in and exhaling whilst telling myself that the power was in me. I imagined myself in a calm tranquil environment, filled with trees and grass and lakes. The dread started to ease, I regained control of myself. I opened my eyes, I felt better. I then had an urge to go for a walk in the park. I guess I just wanted to keep the tranquil feeling and be around nature. This was my decision, I chose to go to the park.

I walked down to the park and stood on the hill just to admire the view. It was nice, it was pleasant. The sun was out and it really brightened everything up. There's a bunch of really big majestic trees I like to look at. Sometimes I feel that I would like to be a tree, to stand tall and proud, to be firmly rooted and part of nature. I feel like trees have a lot of wisdom, they live for hundreds if not thousands of years. They can outlive all other living beings. How much they have seen, how much they must know.

My legs started aching so I decided to walk further down to the benches and sit down for a bit. I sat on the bench and directly in front of me was a group of teenagers playing a game of football on the field. It was an eleven a side game using the public goals. I was watching them play and what really stood out to me was how much they were trying. All of them, they were running as fast as they could, they were screaming at each other, they were tackling as hard as they could, when they scored they would celebrate and cheer, when they were fouled they would argue. Honestly I could not understand it. There was no audience, this was a personal game, they were not getting paid, it was not part of a wider competition, there was no trophy involved, so why did they care so much? The game had no meaning, there was nothing to play for, yet each and every one of them cared so much. They put all their energy and effort into winning something that means nothing. I really struggled to make sense of this, I couldn't understand why they were playing. They were playing for something that doesn't exist, but they knew this, they organised it, they chose to play. I thought about going and asking them why they were bothering, but even if they explained to me I probably still wouldn't understand.

I got some more energy in my legs so I decided to carry on walking. I walked further down across a wide stretch of grass and after a while I started to feel tired again so I thought I would sit on the grass for a bit. I sat for a while just looking around at everyone, wondering what they were up to. There was a man walking his dog, a woman pushing a pram, an old couple taking a stroll. About 50 feet from me were some teenagers, 2 boys and 2 girls, around 17 years old maybe. They looked so happy, they were all laughing, they were holding each other, constantly smiling. One of the boys was stroking the hair of one of the girls, the other couple were playing thumb wars. There was not a single care in the world. The more I stared at them the angrier I got. I just wanted to go over there and shout at them, I wanted to wake them up, to ruin their ignorance and destroy their innocence. I wanted to break them. But I didn't. Let them carry on pretending, actors who don't even know they are in a play, how pathetic. The sight of their smiles, the sound of their laughter, it was torturing me; so specious. I got up, I had to leave.

As I left the park I realised that the nausea I felt for these teenagers was perhaps routed in jealousy, I hated them because they were happy and I wasn't, I hated them because they have each other and I have no one. I hated them because they served as the ultimate reminder. I am so alone. I am plagued with loneliness. I have no one to talk to, no one to laugh with and no one to love. I've witnessed myself destroy my entire life and now I walk alone in the destruction. I am all I have, and I hate what I am.

As soon as I got home I sat on my bed and I haven't moved since. I am sorry to say that negative Simon has taken control and I have just let him. I didn't fight, I didn't resist, I didn't counter the negative thoughts, I let them carry me away. Today was tough, I'm hoping each day gets a little easier.

It was around 12:30pm when I woke up. I didn't want a repeat of yesterday, I didn't want to feel anger towards you, you're trying your best to help me and I want to try too. I didn't want to spend hours deciding what to do. I needed to make a quick decision and go with it. My first thought was that I felt hungry - that settles it, I choose to go out to eat. My mother usually makes me lunch and leaves it in the fridge for me, but that was not what I was going to be eating today, no, today I was taking the bus into town and going to **[redacted]** Sandwich Hut for lunch. That was my decision.

The bus was on time, it took 15 minutes to get to town. When I stepped off my attention was drawn to a homeless man, he was lying unconscious on the floor, right next to a jewellery store. I don't know if he was sleeping, passed out from drugs or alcohol or even dead. But he was there, just lying there, not speaking, not moving, just there. Almost like a prop, to remind everyone what the consequences of freedom can be. But as expected with hard truths, people were just ignoring it, trying their best not to look directly at it, they know it is there, but they would rather lie to themselves than confront the harsh reality; anything to maintain their bubble of ignorance. People would step over him holding their cash as they entered the jewellery store. People would step over him holding their precious stones as they left the jewellery store. Subjective meaning had never been so obvious, so painfully accurate and so harrowingly real. Do I really want to live in this world?

I walked to **[redacted]** Sandwich Hut and joined the que. The menu was displayed on the signs above the counter. There was dozens and dozens of sandwiches to choose from, all options spread across a whole wall. I didn't think this far ahead. I was seeing all the options and I was trying to decide, I could feel the dread building up in me again, I started to lose my breath, my heart was beating like a machine gun being fired. I could feel myself start to sweat. I closed my eyes, I took a deep a breath, I had to tell myself I was in control, I had to calm down. As I was trying to take control I heard the cashier scream "Next" I was still paralysed. "Next!" I couldn't move. "Excuse me sir, would you like to order?" It was me, it was my turn, I needed to decide, I needed to act, now it had to be now! "Sir, can you hear me? Would you like to order?" I opened my eyes but I still couldn't speak, I was struggling to breathe, I was frozen, the dread had taken over, I could feel it gripping my chest, it was beating me. I felt someone tap me on the back "I think you're up mate", I could see that everyone was looking at me, waiting for me, all my problems, all my issues, everything that is wrong with me was on display for the whole shop to see. "Sir I am gonna need you to order or please step out of the way." I was still frozen. I could then hear a voice telling me to run, to get out as fast as I could, get away from the spotlight, back into the lonely shadows where you belong. I regained some feeling in my legs, I am not sure if I had even decided to or not, it's like my body took control of itself, but before I knew it I was running out the store. I'm sorry, I failed again.

I went and sat on a bench for a bit, I had to get my breath back, I had to calm down. I felt myself slowly come back, slowly regain control. I went home and I had the lunch my mum made for me. Simple and easy, it was there, ready, made, decided for me.

From: Simon@**[redacted]**
Sent: 04/06/2022 - 23:07
To: Linda@**[redacted]**
Subject: Simon's Journal

It was around 10am when I woke up, I immediately got out of bed, I knew the longer I stayed in the bed the more I would think and the harder it would be to get up. I didn't want another day of failure.

I went downstairs, my mother was out, she had probably gone shopping. I was trying to decide what to decide, I knew my decision had to be quick, I couldn't over think it, the dread will return. For some reason, I remembered a billboard in town advertising an art exhibition of local college and university artists, it was taking place today at the community centre. I decided to go there, I didn't want to give it much more thought, this was my decision, I was going.

I grabbed the bus back into town and headed for the community centre. When I arrived there were maybe 50 people in the exhibition, they were all different ages, they were all dressed in different ways, but they all looked like they belonged there. I didn't. When I walked in everyone turned and looked at me, as though they could tell I was an outsider, I was nothing but a tourist in their world. I could feel them all judging me, wondering what I was doing there, they knew I was out of place.

I wanted to blend in so I began wondering. The first painting I saw was by Alice [redacted] at the [redacted] Art College. It was an ugly painting, a stream of different colours starting from different areas of the canvass and eventually meeting in the middle and blending together. It was called Unity. I hated it, I couldn't see the art in this piece, it looked simple and lazy. I moved on. The next painting was by Sebastian [redacted] from [redacted] University. This was a white canvass with different weird and unique shapes, each shape was coloured in a dark or dull shade. It was called Disharmony of Order. Another horrible piece that had nothing to it, just a painting of random shapes someone has envisaged. I carried on to so see a crafted piece of what looked like the earth made of different bits of recycled garbage, titled RebEarth. This was not pleasing to look at, and it felt more of a social commentary than a piece of art, again I saw nothing of value, no beauty or anything. I must have seen another 20 paintings and sculptures, all were lazy, boring, ugly or simple. This wasn't art. However, all the other exhibitors seemed to love them and I couldn't understand why. Were we looking at the same works? Was their perception totally different to mine? They were discussing the techniques, the symbolism, the imagery, the feelings they were invoking. They were praising the "ambitiousness" of a certain piece, the "significance" of another, or even the "necessity of the work that spoke of our current time". I saw the exact same pieces and I felt nothing, just a canvass and some colours, nothing else. As an outsider of the art world I had nothing to go by but my own feelings, and that's when I realised the utter meaninglessness of this whole place, it too was devoid of anything greater. If art is just about the personal experience then *anything* can be art, and if anything can be art then *nothing* is truly art. No criteria, no definition, no truth. And yet here everyone was, looking at something that didn't exist, discussing something that wasn't there. How I wished I could feel something, how I wished I could lie to myself, just for a moment, just to know what it's like to find some sort of beauty even if it is not real. Negative Simon started talking, he was telling me I didn't belong here, this place was for the ignorant and the innocent not those tormented by the truth. My chest was growing tighter, I had to leave. I started running for the exit, I just about reached the door and suddenly I stopped. Like weights on my ankles I couldn't move, I was stunned by the final piece that was on display. I couldn't take my eyes off it. It gripped me. The piece was by Asha [redacted] from the College of Arts [redacted]. I don't think I will ever forget this piece, like a hot pike it's branded into my memory forever. The painting was of outer space, the whole canvas painted to represent the deep dark beyond, using the perfect blend of dark blue and black. Scattered across the canvass were hundreds of stars, tiny dots of white and yellow placed perfectly, exactly where they needed to be. In the middle of the canvas was a man, not in any huge detail, just the outline of a man, but you could see he was holding a briefcase, an umbrella, wearing a hat and a long coat. The man was standing inside a see-through cube, standing alone, nothing or no one else around him, just the man, trapped in a cube, standing, waiting, nowhere to go, and nothing to do but stare out into the void. The piece was called Requisite Release. I swear I stood and stared at the painting for almost 30 minutes. Negative Simon was gone. I was in awe and at peace at the same time.

I eventually left the exhibition and came straight home; I haven't stopped thinking about that piece since. Did the artist create the art or did I create the art? I suppose when it has such an impact on your life it doesn't really matter.

This morning I woke up feeling quite calm. I got out of bed straight away and started getting ready to go out. I had no idea what decision I was making today but I just felt like moving. It was around 11am when I went downstairs. My mother was surprised to see me up. I had a cup of tea with her and then told her I was going out for a walk. I left the house and just started walking. I still had no idea where I was going, I didn't want to think too much, if I started thinking I could end up in a dark place, for the time being I just felt content in moving forward.

I was not thinking about where I was going or planning any sort of direction, I was just walking. Eventually, after about forty minutes I felt lost, I stopped to try and make sense of where I was. After gazing around me trying to find my bearings and understand the area I suddenly realised where I was and I was stunned. Was this an accident, just a mindless coincidence, or did I subconsciously decide to come here, did the quiet silent depths of my mind take control of my body and bring me here? I don't know, but somehow I was standing outside the cemetery where my father is buried. I haven't been here in years, I don't even know if I remembered how to get here, but here I was. I stood outside the gate contemplating this very peculiar turn of events, I then decided to enter and visit my father's grave. This was my decision today, something I would never have anticipated, not in a million years.

I made my way through the cemetery, it was very peaceful. Bright white tombstones, lovely crafted sculptures, images of Jesus, Mary, angels and cherubs. White rocks, blue rocks and flowers scattered over the graves. When you imagine death you think of darkness, but here it was full of bright pleasing and calming colours. I guess it was designed like this to make people more comfortable facing death, perhaps to remind people of the tranquillity and peace from exiting life, who knows.

As I walked on I noticed a woman and two children standing and crying over a tombstone. You could see the pain in their eyes, no mask, no cover up, no pretending, just pure real pain. It was nice to see. I never see that kind of realness in people. We always wear masks when we interact, we always try to cover our true feelings, our true emotions. People are fake, but there was nothing fake about this. You could see the heartbreak in their eyes, you could feel the loss, the realisation that they would have to spend the rest of their lives never seeing or hearing from this person again. It was over, the relationship was in the grave with the corpse. All the memories this person once had of that woman and those children are gone, everything they ever felt for them has decayed. That tombstone will live on though, that rock is more real than any of our thoughts, memories or feelings.

I continued on and saw an old woman, probably in her 80's, sitting down by a grave and talking to it. I couldn't hear what she was saying but I could see she was in deep conversation. She honestly thought the person she knew could hear her. In my experience if you don't get a reply your words are wasted. She was talking to a stone, on top of a box containing the bones of someone who used to move, talk, think and act. But why was she talking to the grave, this is obviously not the person she knew. Unless she believes the bones are what give each person their essence, but I doubt she believes that. What gives you your essence is not your visible body, it is your ability to think, the way you think and how this causes you to act and move your visible body, the choices you make, the decisions you have reached based on the free thought you have exercised. That's who we are, that's all we are, a series of decisions and choices and nothing else. If there is no thought there is no choice and if there is no choice there is no person. Maybe it gives her comfort to talk to the stone, box and bones, it doesn't matter, soon she will be rotting in the same type of box and someone else will be pointlessly talking to it.

I eventually reached my father's grave. It actually took me a while to find it, I forgot exactly where it was, but I found it. *Daniel* **[redacted]** *1964-2001. Devoted Husband & Loving Father.* There it was, the closest I would get to the man who co-created me; stone, box and bones. I stood and gazed at the tombstone, I wasn't going to talk to it, I wasn't going to reduce myself to the irrational. I just stood and wondered, what would my life have been like if he was still around? The hole I felt all these years that I tried to fill with nonsense of a universe looking over me; that need I had for someone to look after me, to help guide me, to give me purpose. Maybe things would have been different, maybe I would have been more prepared. He could have helped me with my homework, taught me how to shave, given me advice on speaking to girls, told me stories of his adolescence, the mistakes he made, the things he done right. Or maybe he would have been stubborn, boring, angry and abusive. I would have run away to escape his tyranny, ended up on the streets, unable to go home unable to see my mother. Maybe, who knows, I'll never know. It doesn't matter now though does it? He's gone, in fact he was never there, all I have are stories and the odd picture. He is a myth, no more real than any other folklore or legend. If existence is perception then he never existed.

I left the cemetery and went home. When my mother asked me where I went, I just told her I went for a long walk around town, I lied, it was easier than explaining the truth, after all I don't know why I went to the cemetery in the first place, nonetheless that was my choice.

I didn't do anything today, but before you get upset and think I failed I need to explain why. I woke up this morning around 8am and all I could do was think about the strangest dream I had last night. I don't usually dream, very-very rarely. In fact, I can't even remember the last time I dreamt. But last night I had the most vivid dream that I fully remember, every single moment and detail and I haven't stopped thinking about it all day.

I was standing in the middle of a forest, it was late at night but it wasn't too dark. The moon was enormous and really bright, illuminating my surroundings. The sky was filled with millions of stars, I could even see other planets in the distance. The whole universe above had never looked so clear, so defined. Down below I was surrounded by trees, giant trees, branches full of leaves fiercely shaking in wind. In front of me the forest split into two paths, I was standing at the fork looking on at both. Something was telling me that I had to keep moving forward, I couldn't turn back, but I had to choose which path to continue on down. The path to the right of me was dark, I could see as it continued it kept getting darker and darker. There were no more trees down this path, it looked bare, it looked simple, uncomplicated, but it looked scary. The path on left had trees running all the way down, as far as I could see. There were also rows of me standing there, going all the way down the path, an infinite amount of Simons just standing there. Each Simon looked slightly different, some were happy, others were sad, some were laughing, others were crying, some were dancing, others were shouting, some were in a suit, others were in different uniforms, some were holding a baby, some were dressed in a wedding suit, some were reading, some were on their phone. Some looked middle aged, some looked old. This continued on and on and on, different types of Simons lined up standing under the trees, continuing down the path as far as I could see.

I had to move, I had to choose a path to continue on. I knew that when I chose a path I wouldn't be able to come back, there was no turning back, only moving forward. I had to choose, and I had to live with the path I chose. I stepped forward and all the Simons on the left path turned their heads and stared at me. They all stopped what they were doing, all their facial expressions changed to a blank look, they said nothing, they did nothing, they just stared at me, silently, waiting for me to decide. I turned to the path on my right and everything started getting darker, I looked up and the bright moon started to lose its glow, it was getting dimmer, the stars started to disappear. I turned to the path on my left and looked up, the moon regained its brightness and the stars started to reappear. All the Simons were still staring at me intensely, waiting for me to decide. The wind was now getting stronger, the trees around me were moving like crazy, the leaves were blowing off and being blown towards me. They started hitting my face, sticking to my clothes and in my hair. I then heard a loud explosion of thunder in sky. I looked up and again another loud explosion. The wind gained even more momentum and began forcefully pushing me from behind. My time was up, I had to decide. I turned to the left, all the Simons smiled, they reached out their arms to welcome me down the path. But, as I went to walk I realised I was stuck, I was frozen, I couldn't move. I wanted to, I really wanted to but I physically couldn't move. Then I realised something was dragging me to the right path, I couldn't see what it was I could only feel it, but it was there, it was trying to force me to take the right path. I was fighting it, with every bit of energy I had, I tried to move to the left, I tried to take the left path, but this force was too strong, it was pulling me to right, I resisted trying to move to the left and I ended up being stuck in the middle, unable to move. My time was up, the sky roared in anger, I then woke up.

I spent all morning, all afternoon thinking about this dream. My subconscious is trying to tell me something but I am not sure what. I didn't have any energy to do anything else, even to think about anything else. I wanted to stay home, to stay in my room. That was my choice today and I am ok with it.

I didn't have any more dreams last night, I did however wake up still thinking about Sunday night's dream. I think my subconscious is angry at my indecisiveness, I think it is trying to push me forward. I don't know, but it is playing on my mind.

I knew I was seeing you tomorrow so I didn't want another day of doing nothing, I had to get up, I had to make some choices, I had to act.

I got out of bed as fast as I could. As I was getting dressed I realised how tired and bored I am of my clothes. Come to think of it, I have been wearing the same t-shirt and jeans for months now, I need a change. If I am going to think different maybe I need to look different. I decided - today I was going into town and I was going to buy some new clothes. This was my decision, and I planned to make the choices on the attire too.

The bus arrived on time and took me straight into town. I already knew the shop I was going to, **[redacted]** For Men, I used to go there often before I went to uni. I got off the bus and headed straight there. It was busier than I thought it would be, dozens of teenagers, young adults even some older men, all rummaging through the racks, gazing at the clothes, admiring themselves in the mirror. I saw a man walk out of the changing room wearing a shirt, a woman who was presumably his girlfriend shook her head in disapproval, he turned around and went back into the changing room. I saw another man try on 5 different jackets whilst posing in front of the mirror. I saw two teenagers holding a basket containing dozens of different t-shirts and shorts. Why do we care so much about what we look like? Why do we put so much effort and money into our looks? Vanity; it makes such little sense, every second we live we are aging, we are deteriorating, we are getting older and uglier in each dying cell. Surely there's better things we can be doing with our time than trying to mask the inevitable ugliness that is slowly coming through. Such is the nature of the fakeness in people. Would humanity be better off if we put as much effort into improving and valuing our minds as we do with our looks? The mind is very much an appreciating asset right up until you are very old, maybe 75 or even 80. Whereas your looks become a depreciating asset as soon as you hit 25. It must make more sense to pay attention to mind over matter. Still, I was here doing the exact same thing as everyone else. I shouldn't over think this, either I give in and buy some clothes, or I follow my thoughts to their logical end and dress solely in old rags and sheets. I choose the former.

I made my way around the shop, looking at the different types of clothes. I don't know why I never realised this before but the selection was so vast. Hundreds of different types of t-shirts, jumpers, jeans, trousers, jackets, blazers, coats, cardigans. V-necks, round necks, skinny fit, slim fit, baggy, X brand, Y brand, Z brand, A brand on and on and on it went. How could there possibly be so much selection in one shop, why is there this much choice? How can I know what looks best on me with such a huge selection? How do I know if I am buying the right clothes? What if none of these are the right clothes for me? It is impossible to know, it is impossible to choose in an endless pit of options. Negative Simon started talking. I am not cut out for this. No matter how nice our clothes are, how beautiful we will look, it's always on a timer, essentially we are just decaying matter, so what's the point in even trying. My chest was getting tighter, the clothes felt like they were closing in on me, smothering me, I was struggling to breath. There it was, right on time. Negative Simon had control and the dread was returning, building, building, building up; it had taken over me. My heart was racing, I started sweating, I started shaking. I had to get out, if I didn't get out I was going to suffocate, I was going to die. I could see the exit, it was moving further and further away from me, but if I ran fast enough I could just about reach it. Now! I had to run now, my life depended on it! I was just about to run but I stopped myself. A faint voice in my head was telling me to remember, reminding me where the true power was. I closed my eyes, I took a deep breath in and exhaled "the dread is in me". I took a deep breath in and exhaled, "I am in control". I took a deep breath in and exhaled "the power is in my mind". I took a deep breath in and exhaled "I control negative Simon". I took a deep breath in and exhaled "the meaning belongs in me".

I opened my eyes, everything felt slower, everything felt calm. The dread was gone, I was back in control. I didn't move, not yet, I just looked around. I took in the environment, the hundreds and hundreds of clothes that were surrounding me. It was magnificent, I started to understand it. The choices are there to give people more freedom in creating themselves, we are here to find the ingredients to build who we are and develop our meaning. It's my responsibility to create myself, I need to forge Simon. And here I was, surrounded by options to help me create me. I was in control of my life. I managed to start moving, I continued round the store. I was struck by a lovely light blue t-shirt with hints of white on the chest, and a pair of very attractive blue denim jeans to match, and to finish it off a stunning pair of white trainers. They all caught my eye but the choice was mine, I bought them and I was happy with my purchase.

This may seem like the smallest thing to most people but I was really proud of myself today. I feel like I slayed a dragon, like I climbed the tallest mountain, like I conquered the world. I actually think I was smiling on the bus ride home. I haven't smiled in ages, it felt good.

8th June 2022

Patient: Simon **[redacted]**

Session Number 7

I have been reading Simon's emails every night as and when I receive them. I was very happy to see the progress over the week. As expected it started off tough, on Thursday Simon was struggling to make any sort of decision, he was angry that he was being forced to choose and was consumed by negative thoughts. Although he manged to go to the park the negative thoughts followed him, his depression was present and his day was completely dominated by feelings of misery, sorrow and loneliness. Friday, we saw a further regression, his existential and philosophical ruminations were present and he seemed to have another anxiety attack in the sandwich shop. His fight or flight response was once again triggered. However on Saturday, Simon showed more decisive improvement by attending the art gallery. His self-consciousness and negative thoughts were dominating his mind, however the admiration and awe expressed for the final painting seemed to calm him and bring him to a better place, he was then able to take control of his fight or flight response. Sunday was a peculiar turn of events and something I needed to discuss in the coming session. I felt visiting his father's grave may have brought up some complicated feelings that Simon was struggling to process. I was expecting there to be a day or two when Simon decided not to act so I wasn't surprised when I read Monday's log, although Simon did go into detail about the dream he had the evening before and again this is something I needed to raise in the coming session. Finally, we came to Tuesday where I feel Simon made the most progress since beginning his therapy. Simon displayed stronger decision-making abilities in both choosing to go shopping and choosing the new clothes. Simon also showed his power in silencing the negative thoughts and controlling his anxiety, again he controlled the fight or flight response and stayed in the clothing shop until he had finished his shopping. The fact Simon decided he needed new clothes also shows a change in mood and a desire to carry on improving. These are all positive signs and an indication that Simon is in a great position to continue building.

Simon arrived today wearing the new clothes he had bought yesterday. I was shocked to see him wearing something other than the grey t-shirt and grey jeans, in almost two months of sessions this is the first time I have seen him in different attire. As he entered the room he greeted me, looking me straight in the eyes as he sat down. Again, this is the first time I have seen this behaviour, usually Simon will sit down and look at the floor. Simon wasn't exactly smiling but he didn't have the usual cold emotionless expression either. His eyes looked less puffy, there was more life in them. These are all signs of improvement and very positive to see.

I asked how Simon was feeling today and he said he felt ok, he felt better than he did at the beginning of the week. I asked why that was and he explained that yesterday's events were a big accomplishment for him. I congratulated him on completing the homework and succeeding at the task. This was what I was hoping to see.

I asked Simon how he was getting on with the medication and if he is taking it and taking it regularly. He confirmed that he was. He asked when he would start to see if it was working. I said that I believed it may have already started helping, but again I stressed the importance of sticking to the recommended dose every day. Simon agreed.

I pulled up Simon's previous emails from past week and we started to discuss them. He agreed that on Thursday and Friday he let the negative thoughts get to him and he was very disappointed. I reassured him that it is common for the negativity to win sometimes, the key is not to let it win most of the time.

"We are human, we have up days and down days, this is completely normal. But when you start having more down days than up days, this is when you have a problem. By getting your negative thoughts under control you will be in a better position to have more up days, and your experience will be a lot more worthwhile". Simon nodded in agreement.

I moved on to Saturday; I said his ability to control his anxiety attacks and not run away was superb and he should be proud of that. I could see a faint smile in the corner of his mouth. I mentioned that the last painting in the gallery really helped calm his nerves, I asked why he thought that was.

"I just felt like I was the guy in the painting, I guess it was like I was looking at myself. Trapped and free, alone in the void. It calmed me. It just made me feel comfortable to know that I am not the only one who feels like this, what I feel is real and exists in others too. I don't know why, this just made me feel better."

I told him to make sure he remembers this in the future whenever he feels the dread returning, he will always be able to beat it. I then moved on to Sunday, I asked him how he felt returning to his father's grave, Simon just shrugged. I asked him if it created any negative feelings he may be struggling to process. Simon just shook his head. I asked if it perhaps created any feelings of abandonment, or anything of the sort.

"I have no perception, thoughts or experience of him so there's nothing to feel."

I told him that if any of his negative thoughts stem from this experience he should discuss them with me so we can help manage them. Simon agreed. I then asked Simon what he thought the dream he had that evening meant to him.

"I am still not 100% sure, but I guess it is along the lines of moving forward, if I am noticing an improvement in myself and my thoughts I need to carry on and not let myself be stuck in limbo."

"Do you feel you are improving?" I asked.

"Before I started this, all I was doing was staying in my room and sleeping. Negative thoughts constantly consumed my waking life. When I started CBT I realised I was unable to make even the most basic decision. Last week I got out of the house near enough every day, I made decisions, I created some experiences, I felt inspired, I felt calmer. I feel like some of my motivation is back. I want to carry on moving forward, I want to start building better experiences and creating my own meaning."

This was great to hear, Simon is recognising the improvement he has made. In my experience this motivates patients to carry on, to try even harder and the improvement from this point on increases exponentially. I think Simon is ready to move forward and we are in a good position to start working on his list.

We discussed all the points again, employment, friendships and relationships. I personally want to focus on Simon's loneliness. He has mentioned a few times how he is struggling to cope with these feelings.

"How often do you feel this way?"

"It depends, sometimes I can go for days, weeks even, without any real human interaction, this is when I truly feel it. It is painful. I don't want to feel like this, I want someone to talk to, I want someone to care about me. But then the thought of socialising, the thought of meeting and spending time with people is equally painful. No matter how lonely I feel, my mind is still drawn to locking myself in my room and staying away from the world."

I explained that this is a direct symptom of his depression and anxiety and it has unfortunately left him isolated. There appears to be a vicious cycle in place, the more depressed he gets the more he shuts himself away from the world, the more he shuts away from the world the lonelier he feels, the lonelier he feels the more depressed he becomes, and so on and so forth. Even though it seems terrifying, breaking this isolation will make him feel a lot better. It will improve his mood, it will reduce his loneliness and subsequently it will improve his depression. I suggested that the first thing on the list Simon should begin working on is friendship, there is already a foundation to work on here. The first thing to do is to reconnect with his old friends and start to rekindle the relationship he once had. Simon told me he always felt closest to Colin, so the homework for next session is for

Simon to call his old friend Colin for a catch-up conversation. I was adamant that it had to be a phone call and not a text message, I want to get Simon socialising again and speaking to people is the best way to start this off. The aim of the call is just to see how Colin is and start slowly working on rebuilding the relationship. I told Simon if it helps he can email me after the session to explain in writing how it went. Simon seemed nervous but said he was ready to give it a go.

I have been putting off calling Colin all week. I tried so many times, I pulled out my phone, I hovered over his name, but I couldn't press the button. Each time I tried and each time I failed. Every single time I ended up burying my face in the pillow and eventually falling asleep. That's all I have been doing all week. I wake up, I think about the homework task, I try, I fail, and it knocks me down for the rest of the day.

I have been really trying to understand why I cannot bring myself to speak to Colin. This is probably my best friend who I believe to be a very nice person. I think part of it is that I am just rusty, I haven't called anyone on the phone in over 2 years, I haven't spoken to anyone other than you and my mum, in over 2 years. I am scared I have forgotten how to socialise, I have forgotten how to be around other people, how to do small talk, how to pretend to care about their lives.

Another reason could be that I have had nothing going on in my life for so long I don't actually have anything to talk about. I'm sure Colin can talk to me about his job, his new apartment, his latest holiday, but what happens when he asks me "what's been going on with you?" What do I say? Do I talk about my depression, how I've spent close to 15 hours a day sleeping for the past y

ear, do I talk about my therapy, that I am doing weekly behavioural therapy to make life just a little more bearable. Do I talk about my anti-depressants, the fact that my life is so terrible I need to be medicated just to make it through the day. Or how about I discuss my anxiety attacks and the fact that I cannot make a simple decision, and when I am confronted by a choice most people don't even think about I have a complete melt down and stop breathing. What do I say? What do I talk about?

I suppose I can talk about my revelation right. Shall I tell Colin how life has no purpose, how life has no meaning, how nothing we say or do really matters. That soon we are going to be decaying in a wooden box, that everything we ever loved or cared about will be gone. The life time of memories we developed will be erased, every smile, frown, tear or laugh was for nothing. Shall I remind Colin that he is not here for a reason, that he is just an accident, a random creation born into the chaos? That neither he nor anything around us is meant to be here. That we spend our whole lives asking, "What is the goddamn point?" Only to discover there was never a point to begin with. Shall I tell him that, shall I destroy Colin's life the way I destroyed mine?

Or maybe I am just embarrassed. Colin was my friend, we were going through the excitement of university. We used to discuss our grades, our future job opportunities, our ambitions, our travel plans. We spoke about how happy we were that we had met, how glad we were to have found a good friendship, how we planned on house sharing after university. And suddenly I just left, I stopped talking to him, I stopped returning his calls, I didn't even say goodbye to him. I just disappeared. I didn't even have the respect and decency to tell him I was having personal problems, I just erased him from my life. Meanwhile Colin has gone on to create some sort of life for himself. All the things we discussed he is fulfilling, and I have nothing but emptiness, a lack of motivation and a heart of sorrow and self-pity.

I also think a part of me is scared. What if Colin rejects my outreach, what if he is angry with how I walked out on our friendship? What if he has moved on, he has no time for me, he has other friends now, friends that do try, friends that don't disappear for no reason. Or, and this thought really does hurt, what if he has no use for a depressed friend struggling to live day to day. What if he doesn't want the reminder of how cruel life really is? Just like the homeless man I saw last week, what if Colin just steps over me. Why would he put up with me, I will just be a burden to his life, a bothersome truth that he would rather not have to deal with. It's easier to push me to one side and pretend I am not there.

I am sorry Linda. I know you were waiting for my email on how the phone call went with Colin and you are probably very disappointed to be reading this, but I couldn't do it, I couldn't bring myself to make the call. For all the reasons above, I don't think I deserve Colin's friendship. I did try, you must believe me, I really did try.

15th June 2022

Patient: Simon **[redacted]**

Session Number 8

I was disappointed to read Simon's email last night, but it is not totally unexpected to have this sort of setback, but indeed this is a setback. At the end of last session Simon seemed quite optimistic and motivated, perhaps he was still excited from his success the day before. His recent journal log showed the same over thinking, leading to negative thoughts and feelings and of course manifesting as inaction and sleeping. Simon did open up very well in the email and I can see exactly what the negative thoughts are saying. His reluctance to call Colin is centred mainly around fear and embarrassment. Fear of rejection and fear that he is no longer deemed a valuable friend, and embarrassment of the mental health problems he has been suffering with. This is Simon's high self-conscious facet coming through so the plan for this session was to firstly reassure Simon that he has nothing to feel embarrassed or ashamed about regarding his mental health. Secondly, it was to get him to face his fears around contacting Colin.

Simon arrived on time wearing the new clothes he bought last week. His body language was different this week though, he walked in with a very disappointed face, he sat on the chair stared at the floor and immediately said "I'm sorry". His eyes looked puffy, his hair was still messy and he looked very drained, the oversleeping was definitely back this week.

Straight away I told him there was no need to apologise. I made it clear to him that CBT is a marathon not a sprint, there will be times when he trips, there will be downfalls, but he must always pick himself up after and carry on. When I said this Simon looked up at me and slowly nodded.

I pulled up the last email on my tablet and I thanked him for expressing his feelings. I told him that there's two points we need to address in this session, the fear and the embarrassment. I started with the embarrassment. I asked him how he thinks other people will see him if they find out he has been attending therapy for mental health issues.

"Like there's something wrong with me, that I am unstable, crazy, maybe even dangerous. Definitely not someone they would want to be close with."

I told him how outdated and ridiculous that was. I apologised if I was being hard, but I said that mental health is very real, it affects millions of people in so many different ways.

"People have physical health problems, people have mental health problems, they are never something to feel embarrassed about. It is very common, and you are doing the right thing by seeking help. If people really thought the way you described, then most people suffering would be too afraid to get help."

Simon looked at the floor again. He replied "But at the same time I don't want Colin to pity me; but look at my life, I have nothing going on and he probably has everything and I hate the fact that he might just feel sorry for me."

"He doesn't have to, if you stay strong and show you are improving then he will just see it as a minor blip in your life, and that is all it is. Colin will have tough times in his life too, we all do, no one has a perfect life continuously. And for you, this is just a small part of your life where you have fallen, I am here to help you back up. No one has to pity you, no one has to be scared of you. You are hurt and you will recover, it is just life. You have nothing to feel embarrassed of." Simon was nodding.

I went on to tell Simon that he has to constantly remind himself of this. That any thought of mental health patients being crazy or dangerous is outdated and quite offensive, and if Colin is truly a nice person there is no way he would genuinely think this. Simon agreed.

I moved on to the fear that Simon has around calling Colin. I read out his point about abandoning Colin without a goodbye, I asked Simon... "what is the worst thing that could happen if you called Colin tonight?"

Simon paused, he leaned back and had to think about it.

"I suppose he could tell me to F-off and that he doesn't want to talk to me. He might shout at me and say that I let him down, that I walked away from our friendship."

"And how would that make you feel?"

"Very upset, it would be like I lost Colin for good and that he is well and truly out of my life forever."

"What else do you fear?"

"Perhaps, that Colin is not in fact angry, he does actually want to talk but I have nothing interesting to say to him.

He thinks I am boring and pathetic, that he sees no reason to be friends with me?"

"And how would that make you feel?"

"Again I would be very sad, it would make me feel like I have lost him forever."

"And supposing that either of these scenarios take place, how would it change your life, what difference would you notice?"

Simon started thinking again. He was thinking quite intensely. I asked again.

"If Colin did not want your friendship how would it change your current life?"

Simon stayed quiet. I waited. I carried on waiting. Eventually Simon responded.

"I suppose it wouldn't make a change to my life at all."

"Exactly. You have nothing to lose."

I went on to explain that the negative thoughts were focused around the worst case scenario, but even if the worst case happened Simon would not lose anything, his life would be the same. At the moment he has zero contact with Colin.

"If you choose to call Colin it will either be a positive experience, whereby you can start to rebuild the relationship, or a negative experience whereby the relationship remains non-existent. If however you choose not to call Colin then the relationship will remain non-existent, that is the only result of that choice. You have a 0% chance of having a friendship with Colin if you choose not to call. But you of course have a greater probability of a friendship if you do call."

Simon thought about this and eventually agreed with me. I then went on to reassure him that I strongly believe, by the way he has described Colin, that he will be happy to hear from him. I said that Colin will most likely be concerned about him and he will be very interested to hear how he is. Simon froze for a second, he carried on thinking. He seemed a little unsettled just thinking about speaking to Colin. Simon then asked.

"But... but what do I talk about?"

I told Simon to be honest, to be honest about everything, his depression, how he has felt the past two years, the fact that he is getting help and part of his therapy is to work on rebuilding his old friendships. I also told Simon to apologise to Colin, to explain why he walked out, that he feels horrible and wants forgiveness.

"Just be honest and tell your friend how you feel. This is what friendship is all about - relying on each other when we are down. Friendship is easy during the good times, it's easy to be someone's friend when everyone is happy, when you all have enough money to go out, get drunk and have a good time. Of course, anyone can be anyone's friend then. But true friendship is being there during the dark times, during the sad times, being there to help carry your friends when they fall. That is true friendship, that is the only friendship. Anyone can get drunk and joke with you, only a few people can let you cry on their shoulder. And if what you say about Colin is true, then he is a true friend. He will listen and he will understand."

We moved on to the homework, and of course the task for this week is for Simon to call Colin. I really do hope Simon follows through this week. As we were nearing the session I made sure to remind Simon not to let his negative thoughts make him feel like he should be embarrassed of himself. Not to let his negative thoughts make him feel like she should be scared. I stressed that he should not obsess over the worst case scenarios, and ultimately remember, he has nothing to lose but something to gain. Simon told me he understood and he will remind himself. I told Simon again that he is welcome to email me after the call to let me know how it goes. I really am hoping he calls Colin, this will be a huge step forward.

I found myself repeating the behaviour of last week, even though your session was so powerful and honest, I have been struggling to pick up the phone to Colin. I would ask myself – what have I got to lose. I would reassure myself – he will be happy to hear from you. I would prepare myself – just be honest, talk about your experience. But each time I picked up that phone I would feel my heart start to race, my chest start to tighten, I would panic and give up. That's been the case everyday this week. But today something changed.

Yesterday I tried to call Colin around 5pm, I freaked out, gave up and I went to sleep. I ended up waking up at around 5am this morning. I lied in my bed staring at the ceiling for a few hours, but then I had a sudden urge to get up. I didn't know what I wanted to do or where I wanted to go, but I just felt like getting up. I got dressed and went downstairs, my mum was still sleeping. I thought I would leave the house and go for a walk. It was a very pleasant morning, I started walking in no particular direction but then I felt like going to the park. I figured it would be nice and quiet at this time of the morning, and sure enough it was, completely empty, completely silent, I was alone, just me, the vast field and the beautiful trees. I sat down on one of the benches and just stared out. Although I was surrounded by such a calm environment, inside my mind was absolutely racing. I was thinking about everything, past present and future. Thousands and thousands of thoughts all fighting in my mind for the spotlight, before I could finish one trail of thought another would start, on and on and on, it was like my mind was injected with adrenaline. I couldn't even tell you any specific thoughts there were so many, it's like opening up the entire vault of your conscious, subconscious and feelings, letting them all escape at once. I hated it, it was physically draining, I just wanted my mind to shut up but it wouldn't. Like a horrible germ, these thoughts just multiply and multiply and multiply, the only way to stop them is to sleep. I started to feel tired, I was about to get up and go back home but the most simple yet amazing thing happened to me. The second before I got up off the bench the most exquisite butterfly floated down and gently landed on my leg. I was a little shocked at first, I know they are quite delicate creatures, I thought it was going to fly away in a second or two, but it just stayed there, perched on my leg, as though it had chosen to sit there, on me, this was its decision and it was happy to be there. I was just admiring this butterfly, it was absolutely magnificent, definitely the most gorgeous butterfly I have ever seen, it was a light blue colour, but the edges of its wings were white, and it's antennas were black and white striped. There was a shimmer of light fighting through the trees that landed directly on this butterfly intensifying the tranquil blue. This beautiful creature stayed there for over 40 minutes and I didn't take my eye off it the entire time. I tried to stay as still as possible, I didn't want this moment to end. As I froze in awe of this sublime moment I realised something special - this was happening, this moment was real, I was experiencing it then and there. Everything you have told me now seems so clear Linda. It's true, all that matters is the moment, all that matters is the here and now and creating a great experience. It doesn't matter why this butterfly sat on me, it doesn't matter how this butterfly got here, it doesn't matter where this butterfly came from, or when it started flying, it's irrelevant. All that matters is that it was there, at that time at that moment to create an experience for me, just me. There I was, all alone in a serene park, the sun was shining, the trees were standing and the most stunning insect was resting upon me. This was truly a wonderful moment, and that is all life should be, that is all there is to it, that is my sole responsibility, to create and live as many wonderful moments as I can fit into my finite time.

Eventually the butterfly started to rise, I watched it slowly hover over me and almost bounce away into the park and out of my sight. I started to see some dog walkers approach me and another person out for a jog. The moment was over, but it happened and I felt peaceful, dare I say it, I felt happy. I left and went back home.

When I got home my mum was up and making breakfast, she was shocked to see me come in, she thought I was still sleeping. She asked me where I was and I just said that when I woke up I felt like having a brisk walk in the park. I sat down and had breakfast with her, she said she noticed an improvement in my mood lately, and said she was proud of me for sticking to the therapy. I smiled at her, she leaned over the table and hugged me, it was a nice moment.

I went back up to my room and felt I was ready to call Colin, I pulled out my phone, I sort of half expected the anxiety to come back but it didn't, I found the contact, but still my chest was fine, my heartbeat was normal, I hovered over his name and still nothing. I pressed call, I could hear ringing but I was calm, I was ready. After four rings Colin picked up the phone.

Honestly, now I don't even know why I put this off for so long, and why I was so worried about speaking to him; it was such a pleasure to catch up with him. I was completely honest with him, I told him about the problems I have been having, how I regret the way I left the house but how I was struggling to cope. I explained about my therapy and my attempt to get my life together. Colin understood everything, he admitted he was worried about me and he said he wants to be here for me throughout my recovery. The conversation did not feel awkward, it was as though we picked up where we left off, like we haven't gone 2 and a half years without speaking. He told me about his life too, he spent 6 months travelling in South America after he graduated, we spoke about the pandemic and how difficult he found it. We discussed his job, he works full time somewhere in the city, I can't remember what he does, it didn't sound interesting. He does still see the rest of the group regularly, he told me how everyone else was, they're all working, Antonio is actually engaged. It was so nice to have a conversation with someone after all this time. Thank you for pushing me to do this, I feel like I am already on the path to rebuilding my world. We left the conversation with a vague plan to meet up maybe sometime next week. Colin left it down to me, he is considerate like that, he knows that I have to be comfortable to come out, he wouldn't want to impose. I think I am ready for it though.

22nd June 2022

Patient: Simon **[redacted]**

Session Number 9

I was so happy to read Simon's email this week, this is probably the biggest breakthrough we have had so far. The event at the park seemed to suddenly put everything into perspective, the butterfly elevated his mood and really made him see and understand everything I have been saying. Capitalising on this positive mood and high enthusiasm Simon was able to follow through with the homework, by the sound of it he had a great conversation with Colin and he realised how his negative thoughts are incorrect and have been consistently holding him back. I am hoping this will improve Simon's thinking from here on and this will of course aid his efforts in recreating some sort of joy and meaning into his world.

I was slightly nervous leading up to our session as I didn't want Simon's positive mood to be just a passing feeling, I really need this to stick. Simon arrived and straight away I could feel a new aura emanating from him. He was wearing blue jeans with a white t-shirt and a pair of blue trainers. His hair was combed. As he walked in he looked at me, smiled and said hello; a small smile but definitely a smile, the face of almost a content person. This was so great to see.

The first thing I did was conduct a mood check, to which he responded he was "feeling pretty good today". This was the first time he has responded in a positive way. I then congratulated him on successfully completing the homework, I told him I thought he done a great job, he really faced his negative thoughts and beat them, and as a result he has re-established a relationship with one of his best friends. I asked him to open up about how he was feeling.

"For some reason the butterfly really made me look at life in a new way. It's like what you were telling me was the theory, and I understood it but I couldn't experience it, and the butterfly was the practise, it actually happened and everything just clicked into place."

I then asked him how he is feeling regarding the phone call with Colin.

"I really missed him, I missed having a friend to speak to. I don't know why I was so scared and embarrassed to pick up the phone to him. My overthinking sometimes leads me to ridiculous conclusions, I can see that now and I can remind myself."

Again, it was superb that Simon has acknowledged this, it will make everything moving forward a lot easier and we can now expect better results in an expeditious timeframe.

Referring to Simon's email, he mentioned that he had discussed the possibility of meeting up with Colin in person, I asked how he felt about this. Simon's face changed to a nervous and uneasy expression, his head dropped slightly and he looked at the floor. I waited for Simon to respond but he didn't, he continued to stare at the floor looking as though he was deep in thought. I asked Simon again how he felt about this, slowly Simon exhaled in a frustrated tone. Still staring at the floor he began speaking, he explained that he does in fact have every intention of meeting up with Colin, this is vital in rebuilding his world, but there is still a part of him that harbours the fear and anxiety around face to face interaction.

"I feel I succeeded on the phone call, I have no doubt about that and I am happy with it, but meeting up in person is a different game altogether. I have to interact a lot more, I have to be constantly aware of what I am doing, how I am looking, how I am behaving. What if we go out to eat and I am confronted by a menu with many choices causing me another anxiety attack? What if I run out of things to say and I start hyperventilating. What if Colin sees first-hand what a mess I am and feels embarrassed to be sitting next to me? When I think about this I feel that dread coming back, I'm scared I will make plans with Colin and when it comes to actually meeting with him I will just run away, and it will be the same old Simon, the one who walks out on his friends."

"Do you know what you are doing now?" I asked. Simon paused, then nodded.

"Letting my negative thoughts take over" he replied.

"Exactly" I said. "This is negative Simon, this is the same thought process that has held you back for so long. This is the same voice that stopped you calling Colin in the first place. And what happened when you called Colin, did anything you were stressing about actually happen?" Simon shook his head. "Why do you think negative Simon will be right this time?"

Simon leaned back on the seat and began thinking. Eventually he sat forward.

"But, it is not outside the realm of possibility is it? What the negative thoughts are saying could indeed happen."

"8 weeks ago I would have definitely said you were not ready, even 3 weeks ago maybe. But so much has happened in the last couple of weeks, you have come so far, trust me Simon, you are ready to start interacting with people. And like I said before, you will have zero percent chance of rebuilding your relationships if you do not try."

Simon paused again, he went into deep thought. You could almost see the cogs spinning in his brain, his mind over thinking into hyper drive. Eventually Simon responded....

"Do you honestly think I am ready?"

"Yes, just remember everything we have discussed. Make sure you silence the negative thoughts, remember how wrong they are, how wrong they have always been. And never forget that you are in control, you have the power, and we know this is true based on the exceptional work you have done in the last few weeks."

"And what if they start taking over"

"Just remember the butterfly"

Simon looked up, his locked eyes with mine, and then slowly he smiled, from ear to ear and then nodded in agreement. It was nice to see. I then moved on to the homework task, it was no surprise that the homework for this week was for Simon to contact Colin and to set up a day to meet, ideally this week and for Simon to attend the meet up and see his friend in person. Simon understood the homework task, he said he was nervous but that he would try his absolute best. I told Simon if he wants to he is free to email me after he speaks to Colin and after the meet up, he said he would. I still like to receive the journal logs after the big events, it really helps me get a better insight into Simon's thoughts and feelings, and I feel it helps him process everything.

I then reminded Simon that next week is supposed to be our last session as he was only approved for 10 CBT sessions, however I said that I would be recommending for his GP to extend the sessions by another 10. Simon reacted quite positively to this, he thanked me and said "I don't think I'm ready to face the world alone". I told him that he has made huge progress, there is a bit more work to do and I will be here for him until he is 100% ready. Simon looked happy about this. I did however remind him to stick with the medication, to make sure he is taking his recommended dose every day. I strongly believe this is really helping him and his mood, and together with CBT we are making great improvement, and I was really proud of what we had achieved so far. Simon smiled, he seemed quite touched by those words.

Greater London Mental Health and Wellness Centre
[redacted]
London
[redacted]

Date: 23rd June 2022

North West London Clinic
[redacted]
London
[redacted]

Subject: Cognitive Behavioural Therapy Course
Extension Recommendation – Simon **[redacted]**

Dear Dr **[redacted]**

As Simon's sole therapist for the past 9 weeks I can honestly say we have seen a huge improvement in Simon's mental wellbeing. When Simon first arrived he was struggling with moderate to severe depression, anxiety, analysis paralysis, low motivation and low energy. As a result Simon had lost contact with most relationships, he was isolated and over sleeping. The last few months of therapy in combination with the prescribed medication has seen a huge improvement in Simon's mood, energy levels, a stronger will to combat negative thoughts and a desire to rebuild existing relationships.

Although I can report such a positive development I do not think Simon is ready to stop the Cognitive

Behavioural Therapy course. I believe Simon's improved state is very fragile and the possibility of a regression is still present. I also believe there is more work to do before I can feel confident that Simon can handle everyday life without a professional to speak with.

Because of this I would like to officially recommend that Simon's CBT course is extended by a further 10 sessions. I believe this will give us sufficient time in bringing Simon to an adequate level of self-sufficiency and a greater improved level of mental health.

Please contact me directly if you have any questions or if you would like updated copies of the progress reports. I look forward to your feedback.

Linda **[redacted]**
Clinical Therapist

Tel: **[redacted]**
Email: **[redacted]**
Mob: **[redacted]**

I just got off the phone with Colin, I felt the nerves coming back as I was dialling, all the usual symptoms, elevated heartbeat, my chest start to tighten, my breathing getting heavier and heavier. That damn feeling of dread is still there, no matter how much I feel I have improved that menacing anxiety is fighting me every step of the way.

As soon as Colin got on the phone his polite and welcoming voice calmed me down. Just hearing him say "hello Simon" in this enthusiastic almost grateful tone made me feel like he was happy to hear from me, that he wanted to hear from me and was pleased that I called. He was at work so he couldn't speak for long, but I told him I wanted to meet up with him and he seemed delighted, I guess he didn't expect me to follow through with the suggestion. We have arranged to see each other tomorrow afternoon for a coffee.

The call went well, however, that hideous anxiety still poked its head up, it still tried to consume me, or at least remind me that it was still there, still living, still breathing and still after control. No matter how much I try it's still there, ready and willing to attack at any time.

I'm starting to stress even more now. I am realising that this dread that I carry, it is not just in me or created by me, it's actually part of me, it's a piece of my totality. Maybe I cannot destroy it, how can you destroy a part of yourself without destroying all of yourself? I suppose it's not about destroying the dread, it's just about controlling it. But what does that mean? I have to constantly be on alert, on guard making sure these negative thoughts do not escape, run wild and completely take over. It's like I am always in the middle of an endless war, one side trying to suppress and defeat the other side with no end in-sight. An eternal battle. It's tiring, it's so so draining. How can I be incompatible with myself? All I want is just to relax and start creating and living a pleasant life, but is this even possible when every waking second I am fighting this perpetual inner battle with myself. What if I let my guard down for just one second, what if the negative thoughts get the upper hand for just one moment? I am terrified that I will never be able to have a good time because I will be constantly worried about having another episode. I will struggle to create the great moments because all I will be able to think about are the horrible ones. It will never end, negative Simon will always be there, I have to constantly try to shut down this horrible part of me through inner combat and pills. This thought is making me upset.

I really want to see Colin, I really want to catch up with my friend but I don't want him to see me in that awful state, to see me paralysed and haunted. I suppose the only way I can overcome this is through practise, and the only way I will know if I can overcome this is through trying. I have zero percent chance of succeeding if I do not try. I will go tomorrow, of course I will go, I have to, it's the only way, but I am really dreading it.

From: Simon@**[redacted]**
Sent: 25/06/2022 - 21:45
To: Linda@**[redacted]**
Subject: Simon's Journal

I met Colin for a coffee this afternoon, it took every ounce of strength to fight the anxiety, every drop of energy to bring me into town, but I did it, I went and I had such a fantastic afternoon.

I'll explain the day from the start. I woke up at around 10am, I had a message from Colin asking if we could meet at **[redacted]** Coffee Shop at 2 o'clock. Just reading this text made everything real, this was going to happen, I was going to meet up and see my old friend whilst bringing all these demons with me. I could feel my chest closing in on me, it was starting, how was I going to get through the day if I was already starting to break down?

Eventually I got myself together and I replied confirming I was able to meet at 2. By now it was close to 11am, I stayed in bed just staring at the ceiling and thinking. I was picturing every possible bad scenario that could happen. I have an anxiety attack in the middle of the café and Colin runs away embarrassed. Or I have nothing to talk about with Colin, we sit in silence for over an hour until eventually he tells me that I am boring and leaves. What if I start going into detail about my thoughts and feelings and Colin gets spooked by my crazy ramblings and pretends he has an emergency and leaves. These and about a hundred other scenarios all swirling in my mind. It was the same old vicious cycle, the more I thought the more anxious I got, the more anxious I got the more I thought and so on and so on.

I looked at the clock and somehow it was now 1 o'clock! If I was going to make it for 2 I had to get up now, I had an hour to get ready and grab the bus into town. But I was anchored to my bed, the paralysis was back, that anxiety had grabbed me and pinned me down. It didn't want me to go, it knew that if I met Colin I might actually improve my life and so it would lose some of its power, my joy weakens these demons and they know it, they will try everything they can to stop me living my life. I noticed that I was breathing really fast, my heart running while my body was frozen. I worked on the breathing exercises, they have helped me before and I needed them again. Deep breath in "I am in control" breathe out. Deep breath in "The power is in me" breathe out. Deep breath in "I need to create the better moments" breathe out. Deep breath in "I create the meaning" breathe out. The demons were quiet – for now.

I got up, I got dressed, I took my medication and I made my way to the bus stop. It was such a bright and glorious summer's day, hot but with a gentle breeze to cool you off. It was

1.35, I just missed the previous bus so I had to wait. I was going to be late. "Typical Simon, can't be trusted, unreliable, lazy, not worthy of friendship, he will just let you down, destined to be alone because no one can stand him." Negative Simon trying to get through again. He was lying, I know Colin wants to see me, he was happy to hear from me, he is taking time out of his life to meet me. "Only because he feels sorry for you, he pities you, deep down he just wants to see what a mess you are so he can feel better about his own life. That's all you are, a mess. Don't let him see what you have become, what you are, no one can judge you if you are alone. Go home, go home now!" - Maybe I was out of depth here, maybe it was too soon, I am a mess, I shouldn't be socialising with people, not yet anyway, I'm not ready for this, it's all happening too quickly, nice try but it's time to give up. I could feel the demons smile. I turned around, I was about to go home, but just then I saw the bus coming. I had a few seconds to decide. I can go home, I can hide away from everything and everyone, no judgement, no anxiety, no fear. But, no joy, no pleasure, no meaning. I can't let negative Simon control my life, I won't have a life worth living. The bus stopped I immediately boarded.

It was gone 2 when I got to town, I got off the bus, the café shop was about a 7 minute walk from the bus stop. The sun was suddenly gone, it had completely clouded over, it now felt dark and grey, the gloom made me feel uneasy. As I

121

was walking all I could hear were the demons screaming, telling me to turn around, telling me I was making a mistake. The more I walked the angrier they got, their violent swipes ripping through my mind, shredding my confidence, my motivation, trying to destroy my energy. But I didn't stop, I carried on walking, they weren't going to win and they knew it. As I was getting closer to the coffee shop they were frantically panicking, the most aggressive tantrum I have ever felt. There was a war going on inside me.

I arrived at **[redacted]** Coffee Shop, I saw Colin sitting inside right by the window scrolling through his phone. As soon as he saw me he waved and smiled, instantly the clouds disappeared and the sun burst out as though it was energised and glad to be back. As I entered the coffee shop Colin stood up, shook my hand and hugged me. "It's so good to see you" he said. My eyes welled up. Here stood a great person embracing me and 2 minutes ago there was a part of me telling me to run away. Those few seconds in Colin's arms caged every negative thought I had, extinguished all my anxiety and evaporated all my doubts. I was in the moment, appreciating every second.

We sat down, Colin had already ordered his drink, the waitress came over with a menu, handed it to me and left. "So how are you?" Colin asked. "Still struggling, but getting better everyday" I replied. I then explained to him what I went through this morning just thinking about seeing him. Colin listened to every word I said, no judgement, no pity, just a concerned friend. He told me how happy he was that I did make it, and that he would be here for me throughout my recovery.

The waitress returned to take my order, I hadn't even looked at the menu. I opened it up, but I felt relaxed, I was in a safe space, the dread was nowhere to be felt. The choices didn't seem threatening, they were docile, I was in control. "Just a cappuccino and a chocolate doughnut".

We spent over two and a half hours at the café talking. There was not a single moment of silence. We spoke, we laughed, we conversed and discussed. From TV and movies, to gossip about friends, to politics and culture and everything in between. It was a wonderful afternoon. It's like we picked up exactly where we left off, he was Colin and I was Simon, the last 2 years didn't change anything. We are still best friends.

Eventually Colin had to leave, he even paid for the entire bill, he's such a generous person. As we stood up to leave he hugged me again, we promised to meet up soon, he even said he was thinking of organising a reunion with old gang. On the way home I noticed that I was smiling, the entire walk to the bus stop, the entire bus journey and the entire walk home. A big fat smile implanted on my face. I felt so happy, so at peace, not a single negative thought. I rebuilt a great friendship today, and I created a brilliant moment. I will forever remember that afternoon at the coffee shop. I battled through the anxiety, I fought off the demons, and my best friend was waiting for me on the other side with open arms. Things are starting to look up and I am glad to be here to experience them.

North West London Clinic
[redacted]
London
[redacted]

Date: 27/06/2022

Greater London Mental Health and Wellness Centre
[redacted]
London
[redacted]

Subject: RE Cognitive Behavioural Therapy Course
Extension Recommendation – Simon **[redacted]**

Dear Linda

Thank you for your recent letter and the update on
Simon **[redacted]**. It is very positive to hear the progress
you are making. As per your recommendation and
progress notes I hereby confirm that Simon's Cognitive
Behavioural Therapy course can be extended by a further
10 sessions.

I wish you the very best in the treating Simon and I look
forward to hearing the updates on this case.

Kind Regards

Dr Edmund **[redacted]**
Tel: **[redacted]**
Email: **[redacted]**

29th June 2022

Patient: Simon **[redacted]**

Session Number 10

More positive news coming from Simon this week. It was really great to read about his meet up with Colin, and although the ruminations, negative thoughts and anxiety were present he managed to overcome them all, he fought through all the torment and followed through with his promise to me and to Colin and attended the coffee date. I could feel through the email that Simon is experiencing more joy, he is starting to develop a more positive outlook and starting to have more confidence in himself. The fact he was able to power through every voice telling him to turn around shows he is getting stronger and displaying significant self-growth and self-improvement. We must now capitalise on this positive feeling, this is the best moment to begin improvement on the other areas of his life. The focus for this session was on moving forward and looking into what new areas we can start to work on from Simon's list.

When Simon arrived he entered with a big smile on his face, he said hello in a chirpy and proud tone whilst making direct eye contact with me. He was wearing a white t-shirt with blue shorts and trainers, his hair was very tidy and styled, he was also clean shaven. Simon sat downed, he seemed alert, like he was looking forward to getting started. This is the first time Simon has entered the room with a big smile on his face and this is very good to see. The interest in his appearance is also a very good sign, his tidy hair and groomed face shows he is committed to improving himself, but more so, he believes an improvement is occurring. In the 2 seconds of Simon entering the room I felt like I was interacting with a brand-new person, a happier more content person. This amelioration is definitely delicate, but it's working and it is fantastic to see.

I conducted a mood check and Simon responded that he was feeling "pretty good". He explained that seeing Colin face to face was a big challenge that he overcame and he feels so much better for it.

"Everything in my mind was trying to keep me from seeing him. My darkest thoughts, the most pessimistic voices, all blocking me. But I battled through them. For the first time in years I had a great afternoon, with a great friend, talking about great things. I felt real again."

He was smiling as he was explaining this to me. I told him that what I was seeing was basically a new man. His persistence every week, the hard work, the completion of all homework tasks, these were all his accomplishments and these were all helping him.

"By knowing you are in control and exercising this power, look how far you have come. You are putting in the effort and we are seeing a significant change in your thinking and your actions. If we carry on like this we will get you to a place where you will feel satisfied, you will feel joy in being alive and you will create the worthwhile and meaningful existence that you have been longing for.

Simon's eyes widened with delight. He smiled at me and asked me what the next steps are. I told him there was additional good news, the CBT course has been extended by a further 10 sessions.

"I am not done with you yet Simon. I am happy with what we have accomplished so far but there is more work to do and I will be right here with you as we continue down this journey of self-improvement."

Simon nodded in approval. We went back to discussing the list. Friendship was an area we have already seen great strides in; however he has to continue to work on it. He mentioned in his email that Colin was thinking about arranging a reunion with the rest of the group. I asked Simon how he felt about that.

"I haven't given it a huge amount of thought to be honest. I think it's quite daunting seeing everyone at once. Deep down I knew Colin was a great person, so maybe it was easier for me to see him, it was safer, he was more likely to be understanding of my situation. But the others I am not so sure, they can be quite mean at times, especially Tom, I've seen him be very horrible to people, while Andrew and Antonio just giggle away."

"So would you not want to go if a reunion was arranged?"

"I definitely would want to go, but if I think about it I worry that I will start obsessing over it and drive myself crazy again. I will awaken that anxiety and maybe I will stop myself from going."

"Is this the same way that you almost stopped yourself from seeing Colin?"

"Yes."

"And how happy are you that you went to see Colin. How much better do you feel?"

Simon sat back and began to think. He then looked down and stared at the floor.

"I completely see your point Linda, but the difference from just seeing Colin, to seeing the whole group is so vast."

"And the difference from where you were as a person two weeks ago to where you are now is so vast."

Simon looked up and smiled. I explained to him that the feeling he feels now will be so much greater when he sees the whole group. He will feel like being part of something again and this will go a very long way in getting him to a position of creating the special moments and memories. Simon agreed, however he mentioned that nothing has yet been arranged so there was no need to discuss this at the moment. I thought I would leave the conversation there. There are of course reservations for Simon to see the whole group but this will most likely be the same routine, eventually he will find the strength to go and he will feel so much better for it. I asked Simon to keep me updated, if and when the reunion has been arranged to send me an email so we can start working on it. Simon agreed.

I moved the session on, I asked Simon what on the list he would now like to work on. He answered immediately and quite confidently that he wants to get back into the workforce and wants to start looking for a job. I was impressed with how decisive and certain he was here, another sign of huge improvement. I asked if he had any idea what he would like to do.

"I know I would like to start working again, to start making money and become independent but I am not sure what I want to do."

Simon has had some experience working as a barista, but since the epidemic of 2020 he has not worked a single day. He will have to look at entry level jobs, but nonetheless he seemed enthused to start working again, he just needed to figure out what he would be interested in doing.

The homework for the week ahead is for Simon to give some serious thought into starting work again. I asked Simon to think about what kind of jobs he would be interested in applying to, what he thinks would fit him well, what he would like to do, and even what he thinks he can work to as a future or lifelong career. I've asked Simon to write down his thoughts and email me. Once he has solidified his thoughts and written them down I have recommended that he start looking online at job applications and come back next week with a list of openings he would be ready to apply to. Simon agreed to the homework, and in fact looked excited, all these signs seem very promising and I am confident we will see continuous improvement week to week. I am looking forward to the next 10 sessions.

From: Simon@**[redacted]**
Sent: 03/07/2022 - 00:27
To: Linda@**[redacted]**
Subject: Simon's Journal

Since our session I have been constantly thinking about work and it's been quite a struggle, I really am committed to getting a job, but I didn't realise how tough this homework task would be. I kept on trying to think about what I want to do, and balance that with what I can actually do, and to try to figure out the best route for me to follow.

I have no qualifications, a little education, and very little experience. What am I supposed to do? I need to be honest with myself, I will not do anything great, I will not do anything worthwhile or anything that will change the world. Thinking I could is what led me into such depression before. I need to be realistic, I have no amazing qualities or great intelligence and I am making my peace with that. I am mediocre, I am an average person, I am part of the herd and I need to look for work that is meant for someone like me, a job that no one thinks about, that no one really knows even exists, I will just blend into the background of society along with 99.99% of all other people. I am not going to aim for the stars because I cannot handle another major fall, I don't think I will get up again.

We put so much value on employment and I don't really know why. We define ourselves by what we do. I suppose it functions almost like a quasi-purpose. This is our role in society, this is our contribution to the world we live in. We're all tiny cogs in a gigantic machine, but at least we have a use, there is a reason for us being here. But this isn't a true reason, this isn't a destiny, this is just us exchanging our time for money and that's all.

I always hear people talking about their dream job, they are looking to do something they love, something they are passionate about, something that they care about. What a load of rubbish! I am not going to find a job I truly love, honestly how many people actually love their jobs. Who wakes up on a Monday morning happy to be going into work? Who looks forward to the weekend being over so they can get back to their job? No one. It's a lie to make the reality of work easier to swallow. Nearly all of us will dislike or even hate our jobs, we will loathe having to wake up early every day, enduring an uncomfortable journey only to give up a huge portion of our waking life to labour. When I worked in central London I used to see people getting off the train early in the morning, thousands of them, a herd of mindless zombies marching to their offices, each one as miserable as the last. I would sometimes stop and just look around, it was such a sombre feeling, as though the life was being sucked out of each person. In a way it was, people were spending 8 hours a day every day in a place they didn't want to be, wasting their only life on earth behind a desk or counter, counting down the minutes so they can go home, get a few lazy hours for themselves only to wake up and repeat the same old soul destroying process. Such is the joke of life, we are told it is precious and that we need to make the most of the little time we have, yet we must spend a third of it working, wishing that time would go faster. So why the hell do we do it? The only reason we do it is for money, there is no noble or greater reason, we work so we can buy food, water, shelter, clothes and maybe if we're lucky some luxuries. Dream job is exactly what it is, a dream and I don't want to waste any more time thinking about it. There is nothing I want to do, I just want a bit of money. It's about what I *can* do, who is willing to employ me and where can I stand to give a third of my life in exchange for money.

I worked in a coffee shop before, it was bearable, I suppose I can look at becoming a barista again, or maybe a waiter, there are a number of restaurants in town, it's an easy commute. I could maybe look at some sort of office job, I do have 3 A-Levels, I can get an entry level position. It will probably be very boring but maybe the money will be good.

I will take a closer look online and can come back with some options.

6th July 2022

Patient: Simon **[redacted]**

Session Number 11

Simon did give a lot of thought into the homework task this week. What initially concerned me about his email was that it was more pessimistic than I was hoping for. I understand Simon's fantasies and beliefs of greatness contributed to his depression, but I don't want Simon actively avoiding any attempt to achieve something worthwhile through fear of failure. This idea that he is mediocre may hinder him in trying to achieve anything special or remarkable and this is not really a good thing. Whilst it is good for Simon to be more realistic in what he wants out of life, dismissing any attempt to accomplish something outside of the mundane is very unfortunate. This was something I was keen raise in our upcoming session.

Simon entered the room with a pleasant smile, his hair was tidy, he was wearing blue shorts with a blue t-shirt and white trainers. He was carrying a folder containing a number of papers, I figured these were the job applications he had been researching. He sat down once again eager to get the session underway. As he took a seat he opened his folder and said "I've been really busy these past few days, take a look at…" I immediately stopped him…

"We will get round to discussing the previous homework task but there are a few other things I would like to discuss first."

I conducted a mood check to which he replied that he felt ok, in fact "a little excited". I then said I wanted to discuss the email he had previously sent me.

"As always I am very happy with your effort in completing the homework tasks and they are indeed paying off. However I wanted to discuss with you something in your previous email. The idea that you do not want to think about a dream job, doing something you love or trying to do something great, this is not the best way to think."

Simon went on to explain that he didn't want to fool himself anymore. The belief that he is great is what got him into this horrible depressed state in the first place.

"I can't help but believe if I was more honest with myself, or if someone was more honest with me growing up, I would have had a more realistic outlook of my life, and when the truth hit me it wouldn't have hurt so much. I don't want that mistake again. If I aim low I will not be disappointed."

I told him that there is a huge difference between believing that the universe has given you a grand purpose vs wanting to achieve something worthwhile. The latter can become a personal purpose, something you strive for that will make you happy.

"If you have your own goal, something you want to achieve, something that will make you happier in your finite time here on earth, then by all means go for it. Turn this into your own purpose, the purpose you created for yourself. If you try and succeed you will have fulfilled your self-fashioned destiny. If you fail you will be in the same position you were in if you had never tried, just maybe a little wiser. Do not waste your talent, do not give up before you have even tried."

"But I do not even know what I want to do yet, I am still figuring that out."

"That's fine, and of course you should work within your abilities, but to completely dismiss the idea of doing something you care about, or love, is a mistake. Whatever that may be, if you find your dreams you must go for them. And what these past 10 weeks have shown is that when you put your mind to something you create excellent results."

With an inspired expression Simon nodded in agreement. We moved on to the applications that Simon had brought. As mentioned in his email there were a number of positions for waiting staff at a restaurants, some barista positions, but what Simon seemed most excited about was a handful of office assistant and telemarketing positions for corporate companies based in the city. Simon said that he thought he would work well in an office and there would hopefully be more scope for progression in a corporate city company. These roles were entry level so required little to no experience. I asked Simon what he planned to apply for. He told me that he would be applying to all of them to maximise his chances of success. I asked how this whole process was making him feel.

"Excited, slightly nervous, but I need to manage my expectations as well. There is still a part of me, that voice, every now and again it pops up to tell me I am useless, worthless, that no one will ever in their right mind offer me a job. When I hear that voice it throws me off my feet for a bit. But thankfully that voice is getting quieter and quieter each day. I just pray that it doesn't poke its ugly head up to scare me off completing the application, or worse still on the day of an interview and derail my efforts."

Of course the negative voices have not completely gone, but Simon seems to be successfully getting them under control and each week they are becoming weaker. I told Simon that if he carries on working like he has done these past few months the voices will be negligible, they will have zero effect on his day to day life.

The homework task was for Simon to complete and send off all of the job applications. I told him to watch out for the negative thoughts and to battle them off if they start speaking.

"You are becoming a master in defeating these negative thoughts, you are taking full control over your life. There is nothing to stop you so don't worry. I cannot promise they will not try to come back, but I can promise that you have the power to smash them down."

Simon laughed. He told me he would send every application this week and he thanked me for the advice.

Before we ended the session I asked if there was anything else he wanted to quickly discuss. Simon did in fact bring up his medication, this was not something I was actually expecting. Simon explained that he was getting a bit fed up having to take the medication every day, sticking to the routine and making sure never to forget. He asked when I thought he would be well enough to stop taking the pills. I told Simon that one day, hopefully soon, we can look at possibly reducing the medication, but not just yet. I explained that the improvement in mood and motivation lately is down to the medication in combination with the therapy. This has all been helping Simon out a lot and it would be a mistake to stop the medication right when we are seeing such great results. I stressed the absolute importance of maintaining with the prescribed dosage. Looking a little disappointed Simon agreed he would.

I wanted to let you know that Colin called me today and the reunion has been arranged for Saturday 16th. Colin, Tom, Andrew and Antonio are all available and agreed to meet at the **[redacted]** Pub in the City. Colin even said that the rest of the group are looking forward to seeing me, and they're excited about the full gang getting back together. I agreed to go, but I am feeling really uneasy about it. When Colin said that the others are looking forward to seeing me I felt all the nerves and anxiety start rushing back. Why are they excited to see me, what are they expecting? I bet they have these images of a crazy deranged lunatic that they can just laugh at.

I asked Colin how much they knew about my situation. He said that they are aware I have had some difficult years, but they won't be asking any personal questions, they just want to see how I am and "have a good time". What does that mean? Am I supposed to be their amusement for the day? Do they all want to gaze and glare at the freak? Maybe they are intrigued to be going out for a pint with a madman, like I'm an animal in a zoo, they are fascinated and want to study me. This made me feel horrible.

As soon as I ended the call with Colin I just crawled into bed. I've been thinking about this reunion all day. I don't think any good will come of it. I will say something stupid, or do something stupid and everyone will end up laughing at me. I can feel these damn demons will get the better of me, I will be a nervous wreck and will probably end up destroying the recently restored relationship with Colin.

I don't know if it's worth it. I may call Colin back and cancel. But if I do I know I will be letting you down as well. I actually don't know what to do. This is a lot for me to handle. Every step of progress comes with an excruciating internal battle. I don't know if I can win this one.

13th July 2022

Patient: Simon [redacted]

Session Number 12

Today was a very interesting and quite a surprising session. After receiving Simon's email early this week I read that the reunion is to be going ahead and it was clear Simon was having big reservations about attending. Initially I imagined Simon would be obsessing over the meet up all week, causing him a lot of anxiety, reigniting his depression and leading to him oversleeping again. This was going to be the main focus of the session ahead, I had to try to help him overcome the expected negative thoughts.

I was waiting for Simon to arrive looking untidy and drowsy. To my surprise Simon arrived with some energy. He was wearing black tracksuit bottoms, black plimsolls with a white t-shirt and his hair was combed and styled, again he looked freshly shaved. He made eye contact and smiled as he walked in. I knew then that this wasn't going to be as bad as I initially anticipated.

As soon as Simon sat down he started off the conversation by apologising for his email. I told him there was no need to apologise, he had done nothing wrong and it was good and healthy for him to express his feelings. Simon interrupted me and insisted on sticking to his apology.

"I think I overreacted. As soon as I got the call from Colin I emailed you, I think this was the peak of my anxiety, negative Simon had the keyboard. But, as soon as I calmed down, thought about it, and processed it all I felt a lot better about the situation."

This was very impressive to see. Simon was able to calm himself down, to make himself feel better. This is showing self-sufficiency and a stronger and quicker ability to overcome the negative thoughts and anxiety. I asked Simon how he was now feeling about meeting up with the group.

"Don't get me wrong I am still very nervous, and I know I am going to be battling with my inner demons the whole time leading up to Saturday. I believe I said in my email that I was considering not going, but I take that back and I am sorry I said that to you. I will definitely be going, although I am still worrying."

"What is worrying you the most about going?"

"It's the same old thoughts - everyone will be laughing at me, that I will make a fool of myself. That my mind will paralyse me, I will look like a freak in front of all my friends. But these are the same thoughts I had before I called Colin, and before I met with Colin. Each time I stress myself out to the point of running away, but when I follow through I feel so much happier afterwards."

Hearing this really shows how far Simon has come. Each experience has made him stronger, his level of self-awareness and self-understanding has developed immensely. I made this clear to Simon.

"You are now familiar with how your negative thoughts work and how your anxiety is triggered and you are able to see past it, you are able to see the bigger picture and you know what you need to do to succeed every time. What you have said to me today and how you have reacted to this reunion shows that you are someone who is becoming a master of their own life."

Simon giggled and nodded. He then told me that the demons will not be going down without a fight, travelling into the city, meeting with a group of friends that he hasn't seen in years is now going to be the biggest challenge he has faced since starting therapy. He agreed that he is ready, but equally the negative thoughts might still get the better of him. I had to try my best to eliminate any inkling that they could beat him, if I could make him feel confident in himself he is more likely to follow through.

"There is not a doubt in my mind that you will silence the anxiety and continue on your, so far, very successful mission in creating a worthwhile life, a life full of great moments, a life full of meaning. This is what we set out to do 3 months ago, and we have come so far. You have not given up, you have not been beaten so there is no reason to lose any confidence."

Simon's eyes were glued onto mine, he was taking in every word I was saying. I reminded him how these demons he refers to only ever lie to him, they evoke his worst fears all to dissuade him from improving himself. When he first started coming the demons consumed him, but the more he improves the less control they have over him.

"If you meet up with the group, have a great time, and re-establish the relationship with all your friends, these demons will be impotent, there will be nothing they can stop you from doing. Go this weekend, remember you are control, remember the breathing exercises and remember the butterfly. These demons will not beat you. Follow through, see your friends, have a great time, and lock these demons down into the deepest darkest corner of your mind."

Simon stared at me intensely.

"I will."

We then moved on the previous weeks' homework session, Simon confirmed that he had completed all the job applications online, he hasn't heard anything yet, but he will let me know as soon as he has some news. I told him he done very well researching and applying for these jobs. I made it clear that he should not be disheartened if some of his applications are unsuccessful, the job market is very tough at the moment, he just needs to persevere and eventually something will come up.

Unsurprisingly the homework for the week ahead is for Simon to attend the reunion. He assured me he would not be letting me down. I asked Simon to email me after the meet up to let me know how it went.

This was an astonishingly good session. Where I was anticipating almost a slight relapse in Simon's thought processes he showed even more improvement and what was really impressive is that he had done this alone throughout the week. All I had to do was reinforce the positive thoughts and prepare him for the meet up ahead, but judging by how this session went it actually seems propitious. I am confident Simon will go on Saturday and he will have an excellent time, should he follow through with this reunion I will consider this a major breakthrough in our CBT course. I look forward to receiving his next email.

I done it, I met up with the group, I spent the whole afternoon with them and I had one of the most memorable and special days of my life.

I do not want to bore you with how the day started off; I know you will be curious to know if I suffered the usual symptoms, and yes, of course I did. I woke up to negative Simon standing in my mind, front and centre with every single demon unleashed, standing behind him and waiting to attack. This morning it was not a battle, it was a full-blown war. This dark army in my mind unloaded everything in its arsenal, it tried everything to stop me from going, it put all its energy to incapacitate me. I won't go through it all in detail because it doesn't matter anymore, all that matters is that I won, I beat the demons back, I knocked out negative Simon and boy does it feel good!

After a very intense inner conflict I found myself outside the station a few minutes' walk from the pub. It felt weird being back in the city, I used to work here, the coffee shop I worked at was only a few roads away. I haven't been here in over a year, the last day I was here was just before the lockdown. I remember vividly how the city looked - it was empty, wilting, struggling to live and just about to give up, it was a sombre sight. But as I looked around today it was a completely different picture - full of life, rejuvenated, it had bounced back from the brink.

I made my way to **[redacted]** Pub, I took a second to compose myself before I went in, a lot was going on inside and I didn't want to ruin the new first impression I was about to make. As I stood outside the pub trying to catch my breath, I became mesmerised by the building itself. I stood there staring in awe at this old-fashioned Tudor type building - white walls with black stripes and patterns and a marvellous triangle roof. I love this type of architecture, it has so much more character than the new modern glass buildings, they're all homogenous uninspired boring structures, but this was grand, this was powerful. But most importantly this building holds on to a part of the past, it reminds us of who we used to be and uplifts us at the same time. When I see this building I am reminded of us as a country leaving the dark medieval times and making our way to the renaissance, it gives me hope. After thinking about this I felt calm. I was ready to go inside.

As soon as I walked in I saw Colin, Thomas, Andrew and Antonio, all sitting around a table. After a few seconds Colin saw me standing and called out to me. All the boys then got up and rushed over to me, they all gave me a big hug and they all seemed genuinely happy to see me. They walked me back to the table, they had a pint there waiting for me. I was greeted like a hero and it felt brilliant. I sat down and I had the biggest smile on my face, then and for the rest of the day, every demon in my mind was silent.

It was such a pleasure catching up with everyone. Thomas is still loud, always talking and joking, slightly aggressive, and leading every conversation, but to be honest I missed having that alpha presence. He now works for some investment bank, he complains about working really hard, but at the same time he was bragging about how much money he has made. He was showing off a new watch he bought, and he was showing us pictures of his new car. Normally I would be rolling my eyes at the shallow and obnoxious discourse, but I didn't, I actually enjoyed it. Typical Thomas, he hasn't changed a bit.

Andrew is now working on his doctorate. Something to do with engineering or something I'm not sure, but of course the guy is a genius and this is definitely the right track for him. He is studying at **[redacted]** University. He started explaining to me his thesis and line of research but Thomas stopped the conversation warning Andrew that he was about to send everyone to sleep.

Antonio is working for a graphic design company. He didn't go into too much detail, he was more interested in discussing his new fiancé. He showed me a photo of her, she was a very pretty girl. Thomas made a crude comment about her and everyone laughed, including Antonio, so I suppose it was alright, I laughed along too, even though I found it slightly inappropriate. Antonio said he has not fixed a date for the wedding but assured me I would be invited. He is thinking of having it in Italy so his relatives can attend but he is not sure.

I could tell they wanted to know more about how I was doing. They were not too forceful or pushy, but there were subtle questions, subtle hints to try and open me up. In the end I thought I would explain to them. As I started talking Colin tried to stop me, he said it was alright and that I didn't have to get into it if I didn't want to, but I wanted to, these people are my closest friends, they deserve to know what has been going on. I didn't go into an immense amount of detail but I did explain about my depression, the anxiety, how it has been for me these past few years. Everyone was quiet, they were not probing too much. I apologised to the group for how I left and explained that I was not thinking properly. They were all so supportive, I think they really understood me. I left it on a positive note, I told them that I have been getting great help from an amazing therapist and I am building my life up again. As I said this they all raised their glasses and cheered. It was a great moment, even thinking about this now I have a tear in the corner of my eye.

After our catch up we had a lot more to drink and ordered some food. We had such a laugh, Thomas as always brought the energy. Around 7.30 we made our way home, Antonio had to meet his fiancé, Andrew had some work to do, and I was satisfied, I was happy to leave this great day exactly as it was. We all agreed to meet up again soon, everyone seemed very enthusiastic about it, Colin was happy to arrange something.

I really had a splendid day. Just sitting there, with my old friends, laughing, drinking and joking, it was a fantastic moment and I am so happy I got to experience this again, only this time I am seeing it though new eyes, I am seeing it in a different perspective. I have been to the bottom, I've seen lowest levels of my existence, now I am coming back up the light has never felt so bright, so warm and so invigorating. I feel that I am back, but it also feels more than that. The things I once took for granted, the things I once saw no value in I have now grown to love and appreciate them. I actually feel a better stronger person because of it.

20th July 2022

Patient: Simon **[redacted]**

Session Number 13

As I anticipated Simon overcame the negative thoughts and anxiety, he attended the meet up with his friends and has come out of it so much better off. I was delighted to read his email on Saturday and I see this as a huge breakthrough in our CBT course. For someone who first came to me with serious depression, debilitating anxiety, lived almost as a recluse, unable to leave his bedroom, interact with people or even make a simple decision, we now have someone who is gathering in groups at the pub, and cheerfully socialising. I am proud of the progress we have made. Today's session - for the most part, went how I thought it would, Simon was more talkative and optimistic. However, Simon did in fact surprise me with some new developments in his life.

He attended the session wearing white shorts, white t-shirt and white trainers, he was smiling as he entered, he sat down and enthusiastically exclaimed "I did it" referring to the meet up. I congratulated him on completing this homework task and I asked him how he was feeling.

"I want to say I feel happy, but it's deeper than that, I feel like I am more in control of myself. I've known for a while I have free will, but the idea of creating a worthwhile experience, and forging valuable moments seemed like something I was unable to do, or maybe just impossible, like I was chasing something that didn't exist. I now know this is perfectly within my capabilities, and I feel like the purpose of creating my own meaning is definitely something that is achievable. I feel like I can live life again."

Simon continued to explain how he now has more energy and enthusiasm to keep building and repairing his life. When we have a breakthrough like this I expect the improvement to move exponentially. From speaking to Colin, to seeing Colin, now we are in a position where Simon is applying for jobs and going out with groups. His mood is elevated and it is consistent, he has constant control over his negative thoughts and the existential ruminations seem to be less, his thoughts now appear to be of a positive nature. It's important we stay on top of this success and try to make as much progress through the list now that we have this elevated confidence and energy.

I inquired about the job applications, Simon said he has not had that much news. He applied to about a dozen different positions, so far two have come back saying that the applications were unsuccessful and one has replied to say the position is no longer available. What was remarkable to see was that Simon remained positive.

"There's still a lot more applications out there so I am not feeling down, at least not yet, I am determined to find a job and I will. I will give it a few more weeks and I will then make another round of applications."

This is a healthy attitude and great to see. I asked how he wanted to approach the list and what he wanted to work on next. To my surprise Simon opened up about a romantic interest. There's new barista at his local coffee shop, he went for a coffee this week and noticed a new girl working there.

"I was instantly struck by her beauty, she had this long blonde hair and gorgeous green eyes, she had freckles on her cheeks, a nose piecing and she was wearing a pink hairband. I was watching her serving the other customers, she seemed nervous and quite shy, I got the impression she has a kind heart. I don't know, it's weird, I haven't felt like this about a girl from just looking at them, but I felt an unexplainable connection."

This is actually the first time Simon has really spoken about any romantic feelings. He has mentioned his ex-girlfriend before but he did not speak of her in a passionate or amorous away. This was different, but again I think it is good to see, this is a sign of improvement, it shows that he is thinking about meeting new people. Of course there were still a few negative thoughts he was still dealing with.

"I wanted to start talking to her, introduce myself, maybe even ask her out, but I didn't, I just ordered my drink and left. As I found myself getting closer to the front of que I realised that no girl would be interested in me, at least not now, my life is still a bit of a mess, I'm unemployed, I'm in therapy and still have a lot of work to do on myself. I can't imagine I would make a good boyfriend now, and I can't imagine someone would see me as a suitable mate, I have nothing to offer."

I think Simon knew exactly what I was going to say but he just needed to hear me say it. Speaking to a new girl for the first time is quite nerve racking for most young men, for an introvert like Simon with the struggles he has faced it is infinitely harder. But still, it is important Simon starts working on this and the sooner the better. I honestly believe it will do him good to at least start a conversation with this young lady. I gave Simon the pep talk he needed. It was a similar type of talk he has received from me before - that he has nothing to lose, that he needs to do this for himself, and that he is capable of anything if he tries. But I also wanted to make it clear that he is worthy of care, friendship and even love. If Simon can see himself as a worthwhile friend or partner it will reduce his anxiety and vulnerability in meeting new people.

To force Simon into the deep end I in fact made this his homework task. I have asked Simon at some point this week to go into the coffee shop and start a conversation with the new barista. Simon looked at me with a bewildered look on his face, like this was an unexpected homework task, but I really think this will be a worthwhile exercise. I told him he doesn't need to ask her out, he doesn't need to flirt, just to have a conversation.

"Find out some information about her and tell her some details about yourself. Just have a conversation, I promise you once you do this you will find more confidence in talking to new people, you will get better at it and it will become more natural. Then eventually you will feel comfortable in yourself to ask someone out on a date. What's important now is we start to break down your barriers. First it was to get you talking and seeing your best friend, then it was to get you talking and seeing the rest of your friends, now I want you to start talking to new people, trust me, this is the next step for you, and it will do you a lot of good."

Simon agreed with my reasoning and said he will give it a try.

Just before we finished the session Simon brought up the medication again. He asked if I had any idea when he could stop taking the pills.

"The longer I am on them the more I feel like I am some sort of mental patient. I feel so much better now, I don't think I need them anymore."

I am disappointed that Simon keeps bringing this up as I strongly believe the medication is aiding his recovery and he is not in a position just yet to stop taking them or even to cut down the dosage. I explained this to Simon and he looked disappointed. I told him that I always have his best interest in mind and I will know when he is ready to stop taking them. I stressed the importance of sticking with the medication and I asked him to promise me he will stick with the recommended dosage. Reluctantly Simon promised. It is concerning that Simon has brought this up again, but I don't want to focus too much on it, for now I will remain pleased with the progress we have made these past few weeks.

I thought I would get started on this weeks' homework task right away, this is another big challenge for me, probably the biggest challenge yet. Although I was really nervous to see my old friends at least there was a bit of history there, I knew who they were and what they were like. Speaking to someone completely new is horrifying. I hate meeting or speaking to new people, usually I go out of my way to avoid people, and if I have to speak to someone new I try to keep it to the most basic interactions possible. I loathe the idea of having to get to know someone, first impressions are a complete farce, it is two people pretending to be someone else, like a mutual audition, we put on an act, we try to impress and then we judge each other's character as worthy or unworthy of our future time and attention, it's horrible, it's demeaning. It's easier to just stay away. As you can imagine it has always been a struggle for me to make new friends, it's a double edged sword, either I find it hard to pretend to care or if I do care, I find the whole ordeal too stressful. And so here we have the task at hand, the more I thought about it the more it seemed like mountain for me to climb. So I tried not to think about it, my plan was just to get it out the way, get it over and done with, if I procrastinated I would certainly freak myself out and fail. I had to do this as soon as possible, so when I woke up this morning I felt ready to go.

I had butterflies in my stomach the whole walk there, I was nervous, but the usual anxiety symptoms were not present, the negative thoughts and negative voices weren't there either. This was just standard nerves, I wouldn't say I liked it, but it definitely beats hyperventilating whilst telling yourself you're worthless.

Although it's only a 5-minute walk it must have felt like half an hour. Part of me was hoping that she wouldn't be working today, I would get there, she wouldn't be there, I could give myself credit for trying but there was nothing more I could do. But when I got to the coffee shop I could see her through the window, she was there, hunched over the counter scrolling through her phone. What's more, the shop was completely empty, not a single person there. I actually had no excuse, this was the perfect setting, it is like it was meant to be.

As I walked through the door she instantly stood up straight and put her phone to one side, she greeted me with a gentle hello, I smiled and replied. She looked absolutely stunning, she was wearing a black apron and her hair was tied into a ponytail, this really showed off her face, the face of an angel. Her nails were recently painted bright pink, she was wearing a love heart silver ring. Such beautiful and delicate hands, I would love to hold them one day.

I stood staring at the menu sign on the wall above the counter. I knew exactly what I wanted I was just trying to bide some time to figure out what to say, my mind was blank, this type of stuff doesn't come easy to me. I was staring at that menu and I lost track of time, I don't know if I was looking at it for 20 seconds or for 5 minutes. I started getting worried that I was coming across as a weirdo, so I asked for a cappuccino. She turned around and started making it. I needed to start a conversation but I haven't spoken to a girl in years, I had no idea what to say, but I had to think of something quick, once the coffee was ready my time was up. Almost uncontrollably, like my mouth had taken over and was speaking for itself I just blurted out - "Quiet day today". She turned around.

"What?"

"Quiet day today?"

"Oh, well usually just before lunch it gets quiet, it picks up again around 12ish."

I nodded. Was that a conversation? Would that have completed my homework task? Maybe, but I wasn't satisfied.

"You're new here right?"

"Yes just started two weeks ago."

"How are you finding it?"

"It's ok I suppose, just doing it for some pocket money over the summer before I go to uni."

"Oh what uni are you going to?"

"I'm going to [redacted] university.

"That's a good uni" – I have no idea why I said that, I hadn't even heard of it. "What are you studying?"

"History and English Lit."

This was perfect, something we have in common, something I could talk to her about, a reason for me to stick around longer. My coffee was ready but the conversation was still going. We started talking about our favourite writers, and our favourite books, I spoke about my time at university. I made out that I took a gap year but I planned to return to finish my course. We must have spoken for over ten minutes, it was surreal, it was intellectual, it was funny, I made her laugh, she made me laugh, I taught her a few things, and she taught me a few things. Her name is Heather, a name just as beautiful as her. Such an extraordinary position I was in; *me*, the person who couldn't get out of bed 3 months ago was talking and joking with a gorgeous girl. What a great moment, one I will hold onto forever.

I done it, another homework task completed, I grabbed my coffee and told her it was great to meet her. I started making my way out. But even though the task was finished, I wasn't. Call it over confidence, or perhaps capitalising on a great moment, but I stopped, turned around and walked back.

"Would you like to go for a drink sometime?"

She paused, she didn't respond. The awkward silence was deafening, everything slowed down but my mind started racing - I was too forward, it was too soon, I should've waited a little longer. Actually I could wait forever there was no reality where she would have said yes. She would not be seen out with someone like me. I overstepped the boundaries just asking her. I've just made myself look like an idiot. Why did I even bother? I should leave, I don't need to hear the rejection.

"Ye that sounds good, let me give you my number".

She actually said that, she actually said yes! She gave me her number and she is waiting for my text! I can't believe it, I actually have a date with Heather. All day I have been smiling and just laughing to myself. I feel ecstatic, I feel alive. I have to sometimes pinch myself just to make sure I am not dreaming, because it does feel like a dream. Me, Simon **[redacted]** has a date with a stunning girl. It's like it wasn't even me talking to Heather in that coffee shop, I'm a new person. I can't wait to see her again, I will text her tomorrow. Every day I am creating new reasons to get out of bed, to stay alive and to carry on. I am filling my life up with value and meaning and it feels wonderful.

27th July 2022

Patient: Simon [redacted]

Session Number 14

More positive news coming from Simon this week. His completion of the homework task is a great milestone in our therapy session. Simon had the confidence to start a conversation with a new person and in fact went above and beyond and asked the lady on a date. The excitement and joy expressed in the email was evident and this carried on into our session.

Simon arrived wearing blue shorts with a blue t-shirt and blue trainers. His hair was tidy, he looked well rested, energetic and most importantly happy. Simon looked like he was bursting to update me on how the week went, he looked like he had some big news. I conducted a mood check and very enthusiastically Simon responded....

"I'm great, what a week I have had, so much to talk to you about."

He carried on discussing his interactions with Heather, they have been texting all week and they have a date set for Saturday evening. They will be meeting at the local pub for a drink. Simon went into detail about how excited he was and how he couldn't wait for their date. On the one hand it is good to see so much excitement and energy in Simon, almost a passion for life itself. However, the date this weekend is a very big deal for Simon, he will be one on one with a girl he clearly has strong feelings for. Whilst it is great for Simon to be getting out into the world, meeting and speaking with new people, a part of me is concerned this could get a bit overwhelming for him, especially if he has such high expectations. Although there has been a significant change in Simon's thought processes and character, ultimately he still scores high in neuroticism; anxiety, self-consciousness and vulnerability are still very much facets in his personality. I worry that if Simon does not get the desired outcome it could bring back the negative thoughts that he has tried so hard to battle away. I do not want Simon's expectations to exceed reality and set him back. I asked him what he was expecting and hoping for in the date with Heather.

"I am not sure, I know I like her a lot, she seems like such a special person. I guess I just want to know her more, build a friendship and see, I don't know, I am trying not to think about it too much."

I actually agreed with Simon's strategy. I explained that this was the best approach, not to put too much pressure on himself or a specific outcome.

"Just go out, meet Heather and have a good time. Do not overthink, and do not over-expect, just take it moment by moment and enjoy yourself.

Simon nodded and agreed. He then had more good news he was eager to tell me. One of his job applications went through, this is for an office assistant position at a company based in the city, they specialise in some sort of IT solution. He was delighted to inform me that he has a telephone interview set up for Monday. He said that this particular application was one he was really hoping would be successful, he researched the company and the role and felt it would be a great fit for him.

"I know I have had trouble interacting with people the past few years so working in an office environment will be a challenge, but what you have shown me these past 3 months is that every challenge I face I come out of better, stronger and happier. I think this job will be great for me. There seems to be a lot of room for career progression in this company too. Honestly I am thrilled, it is like it's meant to me."

It's impressive to see that Simon has this much confidence and determination, but again I felt I had to manage his expectations without trying to put him off or seem defeatist. I never want Simon to feel that he is not good enough and I do not want to damage his confidence but likewise I do not want him to get carried away and once again develop unrealistic expectations about his reality.

"I'm sure you will do great in a role like this, and if you are not successful in the interview for whatever reason you just need to carry on, stay strong until you find what you want. Just do not be put off."

He smiled and nodded. Simon has a very big week coming up. He is going on a date with a girl he really likes and he has an interview for a position he really wants. I asked him how he was feeling facing such a vital point in his life.

"I am nervous, but they are good nerves, they are the type of nerves that you get when you feel you have a shot at succeeding. I no longer believe that I can't do something, it is because I can do it that I feel nervous. I have done everything I have needed to so far, so I am looking forward coming out of the other side of the week a better, stronger and smarter person."

It is imperative that the negative thoughts and existential ruminations do not return at such a crucial time, they could derail all his efforts and Simon has come such a long way. The homework task for this week is for Simon to remain calm, to keep his mind clear, to stay relaxed and keep remembering the butterfly.

"The demons may try to come back, negative Simon may start talking to you again, you need to block them out, you cannot give them any time or attention, not this week, it is too important. You need to be in full control."

"I am in full control Linda. The demons have no power over me anymore. I am winning and I will continue to win."

I hope he stays in this energetic and confident state, it is necessary as he has some very big challenges ahead. I have told Simon he is more than welcome to email me after the date and the job interview to let me know how it goes and write down any of his thoughts and feelings. I am excited for him but equally I am very nervous.

From: Simon@**[redacted]**
Sent: 02/08/2022 - 18:30
To: Linda@**[redacted]**
Subject: Simon's Journal

This was it, this was the week that cemented my transformation, it has been a long and difficult journey, the last few weeks I started to see the light at the end of this dark and empty tunnel, but today I can safely say that I have now crawled out of the void, I am no longer falling though the endless spiral but I am walking on solid ground, I am finally on the right path, creating the world as I experience it.

Since our session I put all of my energy into remaining calm, but there was a part of me that was waiting, on guard, warning me that every negative thought, every negative emotion, every fear and insecurity, every horrible malevolent part of mind was ready to unload itself onto me and beat me into submission. However calm I tried to remain I couldn't ignore the fact that the demons could return. As Saturday was approaching I was expecting their power to intensify. But Thursday it was silent. Friday it was silent. Saturday morning I woke up expecting a battle field in my mind, but to my surprise it was silent. I understood then, the demons were gagged and bound. My confidence, my success, the life I was building, all of this was constantly making them weaker to the point that they do not even have the energy to launch an attack. They were decaying, they were dying. It was just me today and I was ready.

Saturday evening was here. Heather and I arranged to meet at the [redacted] Pub in town at 8pm. I arrived at 8 on the dot. Heather wasn't there yet, I took a seat inside a booth and started to wait. I was staring around the pub, I could tell it was recently renovated, I think I had come her a few years ago, I remember it being old and tired, but it felt warm and welcoming. Now this new makeover has made it sleek, sexy and modern but at the same time it looks cold and arrogant. The smooth white walls, silver furniture and a magnificent chandelier made the place tantalizing but it makes you feel unwanted, no one really belongs here, we all just visit.

The pub wasn't too busy, but it wasn't too quiet, it is nice to have some atmosphere but you do not want it to be too loud and hectic. Most people seemed to be middle aged or older which I liked, the last thing I wanted was there to be a group of young lads, all that would do is pose a threat, either to me directly or to my efforts with Heather. It was a perfect number of the perfect a crowd, I think it was meant to be.

It got to around 8.20 and Heather still hadn't arrived. It wasn't a big deal, someone as beautiful as Heather needs time to get ready, I know how girls are, they need to do their hair, their makeup, there's wardrobe changes. She probably had to text her friends different pictures of her outfits to get their opinions. It's easy for me, I throw on a t-shirt some jeans, a quick comb of my hair and I'm ready, 10 minutes max. Heather deserves to be late.

8.30 and there was still no sign of her. Maybe she was speaking to her mother for some advice on dating. Perhaps her dad was lecturing her about going out with boys, and to be careful. It's fine, I understand.

8:45, Heather sends me a text. "Sorry running late, will be there soon." Of course she was running late, she would have spent hours getting ready, speaking to her friends, to her parents. At least she text me to let me know, what a sweetheart she was. I would wait an eternity if I had to, she deserves nothing less.

9:05 Heather finally walks into the pub. The room lit up as soon as she graced it with her presence. That angelic face and the divinity it carries fills me with warmth and bliss. She was wearing a green summer dress that highlighted the tranquillity of her eyes. Around her neck was a white gold necklace with a diamond pendant, dangling front and centre as a reminder of the luxurious presence I was so fortunate to be around. Her makeup was immaculate, I didn't think you could improve perfection but lo and behold Heather somehow made it possible. Her blonde hair was down, it glistened under the spotlight like a halo sitting above her head, nothing could be more fitting than this. She saw me and smiled, she then started making her way to the table. I was struck, I was frozen, time slowed down and I was grateful. As this extraordinary beauty approached me I wanted the moment to last forever.

I greeted her with a hug and we sat down. Up close she was somehow even more magnificent. I was bewitched, all I could think was that I did not deserve to be here, I was completely at her mercy, she owned me, she could do anything she wanted with me and I would smile and ask for more. I was beholden to her, and she knew it.

The date was amazing. I bought myself a pint of Ale and she asked for a double vodka and coke, she drank it quite quickly so I offered to buy her another, she was happy and accepted. We sat and talked about everything. We have so much in common, we spoke about all the books we have read, our favourite stories, our favourite authors. She spoke about her recent a-level exams and the stress she went through. We spoke about music and films, we have the same taste in all of that stuff. I told her stories about my time at uni, she spoke about her ambitions and dreams. It was unbelievable, at times it didn't even feel real. I had to make myself aware of my consciousness just to make sure that I was still real, still alive and not a character in someone else's story. If I had seen this scene 2 months ago I wouldn't have believed this could ever happen, but here I was, on a date with a beautiful girl, laughing, joking, smiling and loving life.

She finished her second drink I insisted on getting her another. Again she happily accepted, she was so grateful but I was honoured to be the one getting her drinks. I was running low on money at this point so I just ordered myself tap water.

At around 10pm she said she had to go and meet one of her friends. I understand, she is a popular girl, of course she is, she is amazing. I offered to walk her there but she said they would be picking her up down the road. I told her what a great evening I had, I asked if we could do it again soon, she agreed that we should and she said she would text me.

I think Heather really likes me, there was not a moment of silence, not a moment of awkwardness. We were like two halves that found each other, we have always meant to be together and we were realising it for the first time tonight. I think it could go all the way, I can see myself marrying her, I can see us spending our lives together, honestly I think I have found my soul mate, the person I am supposed to be with.

After Saturday nothing can get me down. I have been floating around in a permanent state of joy. The confidence and strength I feel is immense, so when Monday came I was ready for the phone interview, there was no fear or nerves. I wanted this and so I was going to get it and I made sure to project this confidence in the interview. My phone rang at 11am. A man named Jonathan **[redacted]** introduced himself as the Office Manager. We had a very interesting and sophisticated conversation. He first asked me why I wanted the job; I said that I was looking for more responsibility in my life. I then explained that I was willing to work hard and prove myself, and that I was hungry to succeed. I spoke about my previous experience as a barista and the challenges I faced and how I can bring that experience to this role. When Jonathan asked me what I have been doing the past year I told him I was finding myself. I think Jonathan was really impressed, I really sold myself on that call, he must have left the conversation thinking what a great asset I would be to the company, and how I would improve their performance. Jonathan could see that, I know it. He has faith that I will be an outstanding member of staff and I have no doubt that I will be an excellent employee. I will work so hard, I will climb the ladder, and before long I will be in a management position earning good money with a lot of power and responsibility.

Oh how it's all coming together, I can see it all, great job, great salary, a nice house with Heather by my side. I will have the boys round on Saturdays to watch the football, and pub lunches with the Heather on Sunday. What a great life I have built, a life full of passion, great moments, joy and love. This is what we were aiming for and here it is, I can see it, exactly as it should be.

I couldn't have done this without you Linda, you are the reason this is all possible. But I must admit something to you. Now that I am here, now that my life is back on track and I have created the meaning I was longing for, I strongly feel that I no longer need the medication. Every pill I take makes me feel that I am broken, that I am not stable, and that I need fixing or correcting. This was true, but this isn't the case anymore. The medication was for the old Simon. I do not need it anymore, I have grown beyond that. I haven't take a pill since Sunday and I do not plan to, this is my choice. I flushed all the pills down the toilet and honestly I feel great. That part of my life is well and truly behind me, I am looking forward now and my life is brilliant, I have it all, I am fixed.

3rd August 2022

Patient: Simon **[redacted]**

Session Number 15

Today was a very disappointing session and it is unfortunate considering the amount of progress Simon has made. I was upset to read Simon's journal log and discover that he has decided to stop taking his medication. I wanted to use today's session to try and persuade Simon that this was a categorical mistake, the medication was helping him and he needs to start taking the pills again. Unfortunately I could not convince him, in fact I saw a new side and temperament to Simon and I fear things will get worse for him if he does not listen. There is now a risk all the progress we have made will be undone.

Simon arrived wearing a red t-shirt with black shorts and black plimsolls. He was smiling, his hair was combed, he looked excited and proud. He sat down and I conducted a mood check. He told me he was feeling great after such an eventful weekend. I didn't want to waste any time so I immediately brought up the issue around stopping the medication.

"I think you know what I want to discuss with you."

"Yes, the medication."

"Simon, you know I think this is a really bad idea, I have stressed to you the importance of sticking with the recommended dosage, this is only prescribed to help you. I really think you need to reconsider this, honestly this medication has helped you come this far, it is too soon to stop."

"I disagree Linda, I don't think the medication has done anything for me except remind me twice a day of my problems and make me feel like I am a dysfunctional human who cannot live without drugs. No. What *has* helped me is you, my friends, Heather and all the other parts of my life that have given me the great moments and experiences to pull me out of the rut. I am telling you I do not need it anymore."

"Simon please, you need to understand the consequences of stopping the medication suddenly, especially if a medical professional has not recommended it. You're not there yet, stopping like this can cause you a lot of harm, it can destroy the progress we have made so far."

"No it won't and I do not want to talk about this anymore. This is my decision, I am sticking with it and I will live with the consequences, so please stop."

"But Simon, just try to…

"I said stop!"

Simon snapped at me, he looked visibly irritated, the tone of his voice became aggressive. I have never seen Simon angry like this, and it was such an instant reaction. Simon realised soon after that his response was not warranted.

"I'm sorry, I am a bit defensive, I knew you were going to bring it up this session and I really didn't want to get into it."

"If you do not want to talk about it I won't, just remember that I think this is a mistake."

"Noted, but it is not your decision, it is mine."

The atmosphere in the room changed after this. It all felt slightly awkward.

I wanted to move on quickly so I asked Simon how the week ahead was looking for him, what the plans were. He told me that he has plans to see his friends on Saturday for another reunion. They are gathering in the afternoon at a pub in the city. Simon seemed very excited, he told me he did not have a single worry or doubt, the demons are completely behind him, his path was clear to just live his life.

I then brought up the telephone interview to see how he was feeling. Simon projected a lot of confidence and excitement. He is expecting to hear back later this week on the status of the job application. I asked how he would feel if he was unsuccessful, if he would be able to get through it, Simon just dismissed this idea, he said there was no way he would be unsuccessful and he didn't want to cloud his mind with negative thoughts, he was remaining positive.

I asked how it was going with Heather, he seemed very delighted by their date in the email. Simon told me how in love he was, he referred to Heather as his soul mate, and kept on saying how well everything has fallen into place. I asked if he thought Heather felt the same way.

"Of course she does, we are meant to be together."

"Has she said this to you?"

"No, but I know she feels the same way."

I asked how he would cope if Heather did not share the same intense feelings for him. I said that it usually takes more than one date to develop such strong feelings for someone, and Heather might not be there yet. Simon started getting irritated by this.

"Why are you being so negative, you asked me how I would feel if I didn't get the job, or if Heather doesn't like me. I am trying to block the negative thoughts, I don't want negative Simon here, it seems like you want me to be negative, you want me to think the worst."

"I do not want you to be negative, of course not, your confidence and positivity are great to see, but Simon please remember that the reason your depression started was because you had unrealistic expectations of your life and this affected you badly. I just want to manage your expectations here; I want you to be cautious."

"So you think me getting the job and Heather falling in love with me is unrealistic?"

"No I am not saying that, but not every girl falls in love on the first date, and not every telephone interview results in a job offer. I am trying to prepare you for possible disappointments too. Life is about the great the moments, sure, but it is also about dealing with the not-so-great moments too. And honestly Simon, I have been paying attention to some of the language you have been using lately. 'Meant to be' 'Soul mates', 'supposed to be', 'as it should', this is all deterministic and fatalistic language, and this is the type of thinking that led to your initial breakdown."

Simon remained silent. He didn't say a word, over two minutes passed, the tension was growing. I asked if he was ok, he didn't respond. I asked again, and he didn't respond. I could see his lips tightening, his fists clenching, his eyes growing wide, there was a fury burning inside him, this was horrible for me to see. I was getting nervous, in fact a little scared. Eventually Simon leaped up from his chair.

"You want me to be miserable don't you? Just when my life is getting back on track, you are trying to derail it. Why Linda? Is it because you need me as patient, is it because your work relies on people suffering, does the thought of someone getting better scare you. I can't deal with this, I was having a good day before I came here!"

He stormed out the room and slammed the door behind him.

Even though Simon started the session smiling and happy he was also more irritable and bad tempered, this could be a side effect of stopping the medication suddenly and I fear this will get a lot worse in the coming weeks. In addition to this, Simon is actively trying to block out every negative thought possible, whilst I understand why he is doing this I am now getting worried that he is not even considering any possible bad news to come his way, the progress we have made is still fragile and I am unsure and worried as to how he will react should he have to face any negative outcomes in the coming weeks.

From: Simon@**[redacted]**
Sent: 04/08/2022 - 13:19
To: Linda@**[redacted]**
Subject: Simon's Journal

I would like to apologise for walking out of the session yesterday and for raising my voice to you, and for everything I said. I was in the wrong and I am sorry. I don't know what came over me, I guess I was just frustrated, I've been trying so hard to stay positive, to only have good thoughts and good feelings. It felt like you were trying to bring me down and put the negative thoughts back into my head. I've been trying so hard to suppress negative Simon, and for a split second I felt like you were trying to set him free. I was surprised by this, confused even, and I didn't express myself properly, but I know you were just preparing me for the possibility of bad news, and it seems like you were right to do so. I got an email today telling me that my phone interview was unsuccessful and the company are not interested in taking my application any further. I really don't understand this, that interview went so well, I was certain I made a great impression, and the manager really liked me, so I don't know why they don't want to offer me the job, or at least see me for a face-to-face interview. They didn't even tell me why they rejected me, not one damn reason. Imagine being told you have failed and not even knowing why. Am I supposed to just sit here and think about the phone interview over and over trying to work out where I went wrong? Did I say something wrong? Was my tone off? Was I too loud, too quiet? Did I breathe weird? What! How am I supposed to learn and improve myself? Could it be that the manager was just threatened by me, he knew I would be so productive it would make him look bad? Who knows? This is so unfair I am more than disappointed I am actually really angry! And now I have a thousand questions and thoughts swirling in my head trying to make sense out of all of this.

Maybe it is a blessing in disguise, maybe it is best that I do not work for such a horrible company. Still, I was certain this was the job for me, and I was certain that I would have been offered the position. I could see myself working there, I could imagine it perfectly and it felt right.

I have been really sad since I got the news. That drained feeling is creeping back, my energy seems to be leaving me, I am just lying on my bed and all I want is to stay here. I have been here before; I recognise this feeling and I know where it is heading. The less energy I have the more the demons gain strength, they feed off my depression, they suck the life out of me. I can't let them back into my life, not when things are going so good. I must fight them off, they cannot be allowed to gain any strength. I have to try and keep myself positive, I have to think about the other great things in my life right now. I have the second reunion tomorrow with the boys and I am looking forward to that, we will an awesome time like we always do. I also have an amazing girlfriend that I am very grateful for. I can't wait to see her again, I am planning to take her to a really nice Italian restaurant in town. It is very romantic, she will love it, and she will love me for it. I have been trying to arrange it since last week but I haven't heard back from her, I have messaged her a few times this week and she hasn't responded. I know she is busy, she has a job and she is very popular, but still, a quick reply would have been nice. I hope she is ok. I know she's working now so I will call her this evening and try to arrange the date. I might not even tell her where we are going, I'll surprise her. I think she will appreciate that.

Anyway, I need to stay positive, I am upset, really upset, I wasn't expecting this, but I have more to be happy about so I will not let this get me down. I will apply for more jobs, I will get there eventually, I don't need to worry and neither do you. Things will be fine, I know it.

It has been a terrible day, terrible, terrible day. I am so angry right now. The reunion today was a disaster and I do not want to see any of my "friends" again. I just feel like I have to email you and get this all off my chest.

As you know I was really excited about seeing the group again, everything was set for this afternoon. I woke up feeling happy, I pushed the bad news about the job interview out of my mind. I woke up energised and smiling, there was no anxiety or fear, I felt great. I had breakfast with my mum and went back upstairs and started getting ready.

We were meeting at the same pub as before, so I made my way there. We were set to meet at 1pm but I got there at 12:50, so I ordered a drink and took a seat at a table. Soon after everyone arrived. They ordered their drinks, we sat down and the afternoon was underway.

Everything was going fine, Colin was being Colin, Tom was being Tom, Antonio was being Antonio and Andrew was being Andrew. Apparently I was different, the boys said I was more talkative, less shy, and a little louder. I took this as a compliment, I guess it is the new me, or maybe I am feeling more comfortable around them, or maybe I am feeling more comfortable in myself. Either way it was nice to hear that I was becoming more sociable.

The day was going by nicely, we had a bit to drink, we had lunch, we watched the football, we had a laugh, everything I expected. But within an instant everything changed for me, and what was a lovely afternoon turned into a horrible, awkward, infuriating encounter that I had to escape from.

Tom got a phone call and left the pub to take it. When he came back he told us it was his boss and the call was work related. Tom then started moaning about how stressful his job was. He was complaining about how he works 70 hours a week, that his boss is a harsh rude person who has no consideration for his personal time. I heard this last time we met, and I am sure the rest of the boys have heard this plenty of times. Tom uses this sad story about how overworked he is to also brag about how successful he is, it is quite pathetic. But he was going on and on and on. So hearing all this whining I just said.

"If you are that unhappy maybe you should just quit. There's no point in spending a large portion of your life in a place that makes you miserable."

I thought this was good advice, definitely something you would have said if someone was moaning to you. I wasn't rude or condescending or anything like that. Tom then responded.

"It's not that easy Simon, some of us have to work, we can't all have psychotic breakdowns and be unemployed bums for the rest of our lives. Not all of us have the privilege of being mental."

Antonio and Andrew burst out laughing, Tom then started laughing hysterically. I just froze, I sat there staring at them in disbelief; this was actually said to me, can you believe it! All three of them carried on laughing, and laughing and laughing, Andrew even choked on his drink he was laughing so hard. I could see Colin kicking Tom under the table, trying to get him to understand that that comment was inappropriate, but Tom was laughing too much to even take notice. I stared at Colin, he just looked down at the table embarrassed. Everything then started to slow down for me, time had dilated, keeping me in this moment for a little longer, to let this horrid experience linger; me sitting there, with three of my friends laughing at me, laughing at my pain, laughing at my struggles. Everything I feared about seeing my friends was unravelled before me and thrown in my face. I was right the whole time. This is how they see me, this is who I am to them, a psychotic mental person, a bum, a loser, unemployable, a joke. I am beneath them, I am someone they invite out to laugh at, to taunt. If Tom says this to my face imagine what he says behind my back, and imagine how much Andrew and Antonio and maybe even Colin, laugh. That is all I am, their lunatic acquaintance, the butt of their joke, the punchline to their comedy. That is all I am.

As their laughter settled Tom tried to reassure me that this was just joke, "No offense mate, just having a little fun" and he patted me on the shoulder. I am his little fun, my mental health is his amusement, and Antonio's and Andrew's. Colin remained silent, he didn't laugh but God forbid he would ever tell Tom off, no not the amazing Tom, not the leader of the pack, he can do whatever he wants, he can say whatever he wants and this pack of sheep will still follow him.

Tom then carried on talking, the afternoon continued as though nothing happened. I was left to bleed out, and no one wanted to pay attention. So I just sat there, not saying a word. Occasionally they would try to bring me into the conversation, but I was brief in my responses. I stopped paying attention to what they were saying, I was frozen, I was upset and I was angry, but I had no idea what to do or how to react. Were they right to see me this way? Can I blame them? Was this all my fault? Was it a mistake to think that I could ever repair my relationship with this group? Should I accept my new position as the mental circus freak of the group? Is being the group freak better than not being in the group at all? This and about a hundred other questions were running through my mind. All of a sudden the whole group burst out laughing hysterically again. I don't know what was said, I don't know who said it, but everyone was laughing their heads off. That incessant sound that disgusting cackling sent shivers through my body. I could feel my chest tightening, my vision blurring, the dread was coming back, and these 4 terrorists were responsible. Without even deciding, without evening being conscious of it, I was on my feet and running out the door. I could hear Colin calling me, but I didn't stop, I couldn't stop, I was charging out the pub to the train station on my way home.

I got home filled with rage. I stormed up to my room and started punching the walls and screaming. My mother ran upstairs to see if I was ok and I just screamed at her to leave me alone. I carried on punching my walls, my doors, my wardrobes, anything to get this wrath out of me. My hands are all bloodied and scratched. This is what they wanted, the psycho to act like a psycho, am I living up to their standards, now that my doors are cracked and my room as been trashed, do you think they will be happy, am I fulfilling the stereotype, am I mental enough for them?

Colin has tried to call me a few times but I have ignored his calls. He even text me asking me to call him back but I won't. I have been so foolish to think I could've had a good friendship with this group and create meaningful experiences with them. Our second reunion and here I am, screaming and punching the walls, I feel devastated and demoralised. All the confidence I had they have successfully erased. I cannot have them in my life, any of them, they have just created an unbearable experience for me and I will not go through that again. They are out of my life, for good.

This has been a tough week for me, thank God for Heather, her love has kept me going, and to be honest her love is all I need. I don't need that office manager job, I don't need Colin, or Tom, or Andrew or Antonio. I don't need any of them. All I need is Heather, my one true love, she will make me happy, she is the one who will give my life the meaning and the great experiences it needs. I am still concerned that I have not heard from her since our date last week, but I am sure she is fine, she is just busy. I have texted and called her a few times this evening, I haven't heard back yet. I am sure she is out with her friends. I will speak to her tomorrow, I am planning a very special date for us. She will be so happy, *we* will be so happy, together.

10th August 2022

Patient: Simon [redacted]

Session Number 16

The emails I received from Simon last week were very alarming. Exactly what I feared is now actualising. Simon's over expectations are being met with bad news and he is having trouble processing everything. This, in combination with the sudden stopping of the medication means he is not regulating his emotions very well. Going into this session I knew it would be very tough, I was sure the unfortunate news around the job interview and the incident with his friends, would have damaged Simon's confidence, and so I was prepared for a major setback in our progress. Regrettably today's session was even worse than I anticipated.

Simon entered wearing black shorts with a black t-shirt and white trainers, his trainers looked quite scuffed and dirty. His hair was messy, I hadn't seen it that messy for quite a few weeks. The knuckles on both of his hands had plasters. The smile I had got used to seeing was also gone, he had a very serious look on his face, he was trying unsuccessfully to hide his anger. As soon as he entered the room he sat on the chair, his left hand was clenched, his right hand holding the fist. He was shaking his feet, he used to do this in our earlier sessions, he was feeling agitated again.

I started with a mood check. "Angry" was his only response. I asked him why he was angry, but he didn't reply. I asked him again and he stayed quite. I let the silence loiter for a bit, eventually I asked again.

"Simon why are you so angry?"

"Because I have been wasting my time. I wasted my time trying to get that job, I wasted my time seeing those four idiots. I have been wasting my time and I do not want to waste it anymore."

I tried to explain to Simon that he was not wasting his time, trying to get a job was a good thing, reconnecting with his friends was a good thing. Last week he was so excited about both of these parts of his life. I asked if he had spoken to any of his friends since Saturday.

"Colin has texted me a few times, apologising on behalf of Tom, I haven't responded. There's nothing to say, I don't want him in my life anymore."

"Simon do you really think cutting your friends out is the best thing to do?"

"I told you what Tom said, I told you how they laughed." His voice was rising and becoming more aggressive.

"It was an insensitive comment, but from how you have described Tom this isn't out of character, surely you can speak to him, let him know how that comment made you feel, and work on bettering your relationship with him and the group."

I could see Simon's fists clenching harder.

"No way, I will never speak to him or any of them again. Life is about creating the great moments right, and all they did was create a horrible moment for me. I don't want to talk about this anymore. I have nothing more to say about the matter so drop it."

"But Simon…"

"I said drop it!"

Simon snapped at me. I could see the rage burning in his eyes. I thought it was best for me to leave the situation for the time being. I moved on to discuss the job situation and how he was feeling.

"There's nothing to say. I didn't get the job, they wasted my time, I got my hopes up for no reason."

"Will you carry on with the job hunt?"

Simon shrugged.

"Simon I don't want this rejection to put you off trying."

"I don't care anymore Linda, I don't want to talk about it right now, I don't even want to think about it. Just stop."

"What do you want to talk about?"

Simon remained silent. He sat there, his head down, clenching his fists and shaking his foot. Five minutes went by and not a word was spoken. I decided to start a new conversation so I asked how Heather was. Simon instantly looked up at me.

"She is fine." In an abrupt, defensive tone.

"Is she?"

"Well, I think so, I haven't spoken to her since our date, she is just busy. I will be seeing her soon."

"When are you planning on seeing her?"

"I'm not sure, I am waiting for her to call me back."

I am getting concerned that Heather is ignoring Simon, I am really worried that the longer this continues the worse it will be for Simon. I have been getting hints from the emails that he has been calling and texting her a lot and I wanted to tell Simon to maybe pull back a little as he doesn't seem to be getting any sort of response. But, for the first time, I was in fact scared to say this to Simon. The anger and rage he is displaying has indeed made me uncomfortable to do my job and do what is best for him.

"Why do you think you have not spoken to Heather since the date? It has been 10 days."

"She is just busy, she works, she has friends, family, she is preparing for uni. It is busy times."

"Be honest with me Simon, how often have you called her?"

"Huh?"

"How often have you called or texted her."

Simon shrugged. "I don't know."

"You do know, I just need to understand a bit more about this relationship, so please give me an idea."

Simon hesitated, he sighed and then he started to divulge.

"I texted her that evening after our date, but she didn't reply. The next day I texted her about 3 times, but she didn't reply. I got a bit concerned on Monday so I called her about 4 times, but each time it rang through to voicemail. I text her again on Wednesday after our session to try and arrange a date. I called her on Thursday night. I text again her on Friday. I then texted and called her about 4 or 5 times on Saturday night because I was upset and I wanted to speak to someone and I tried again on Sunday night. I texted her a few times on Monday. I called her yesterday night too."

"And she has not responded to any of your texts or returned any of your calls."

"No not yet."

"Why do you think that is?"

"Like I said, she is busy."

"Too busy to send one text or take one phone call."

"What are you trying to say Linda?"

"Simon, I think Heather is ignoring you, and I think you are contacting her too much. You need to give her some space, stop the phone calls and the texts for now, I do not think this is healthy behaviour."

Simon leaped up from his seat, his eyes were wide, he was gritting his teeth, both his fists were clenched tight. He approached my chair; I was very frightened.

"How dare you! How dare you say this to me! Heather loves me, she is not ignoring me, she is just busy. She is waiting for the right time to contact me, she is waiting so she has enough time to have a proper catch up, to give me her full attention. How dare you imply that she doesn't care for me. Why, why, why are you trying to make me feel worse than I am, why are you filling my head with negative thoughts?"

"Simon please calm down, please just sit down. Look at yourself right now, look at how you are talking to me. You have never behaved like this before."

Simon sat back down and buried his head in his hands.

"I'm sorry."

"I am going to be honest with you Simon, I feel this rage is a side effect from you stopping your medication suddenly. I warned you it was a mistake. Please Simon, can you reconsider starting your medication again."

Simon looked up at me, he stared at me dead in the eyes. He did not say a word, he did not move, he just stared at me. After a few minutes I asked if he was ok. He stood up, took a deep breath and walked out the room.

I am very concerned for Simon's well-being at this moment. He is not regulating his emotions well at all. He is now having rage attacks, and this seems to be getting worse every time he is faced with bad news or a negative situation. If this continues it will not be long until the rage turns back into depression and we are in the same situation we were 4 months ago. From here on I will need to go back to basics with Simon, I will need to remind him of why he is here and what he can achieve. I do not want him falling back into the severe depression and anxiety he managed to crawl out of. I am truly terrified that if he goes back into this state it will be worse than before.

I couldn't stop thinking about what you said in our last session. I could hear your voice playing over and over in my mind, all day, every waking second torturing me. "Heather is ignoring you", "Heather doesn't like you" "She doesn't want to see you", "She would never want a loser like you", "Heather doesn't date crazy psychos". I didn't want to believe it, I was certain we were meant to be together, there was no way that Heather didn't feel what I felt. But still, I couldn't stop thinking about it. You were right in your observations, Heather has not responded to a single text, she has not answered or returned any of my phone calls. I was obsessing over this, the more I thought about it the angrier I got. I know if Heather just answered her phone or replied to one of my texts everything would be ok, my mind would be at ease. So I tried to contact her. Admittedly I got a little carried away, but it is only because I really wanted to hear from her. I must have texted her 20 times on Wednesday night. She did not respond to a single message. I woke up on Thursday adamant to speak to her. I called her about 10 times. I even thought she started cancelling my calls, from the 5th call onwards it would ring once and then go straight to voicemail. I was devastated. This beautiful image I had of us living happily ever after was starting to disintegrate. My heart was hurting me, *physically* hurting me. I was sitting on my bed and all I could do was scream, I screamed as loud as I could, a part of me was still hoping that if I screamed loud enough maybe the universe would hear me, maybe the universe would respond and explain to me how it could create someone so perfect just to destroy me, rip out my soul and leave me here in agony. There was no response. Just silence.

I woke up this morning furious. I had to speak to her. All day I didn't eat, I didn't even get out of bed all I could think about was speaking to Heather. I texted her as soon as I woke up, by 11am there was still no reply. So I called her, every 15 minutes, all day. She did not answer once. She did not send me a message, no acknowledgement, no response, just silence.

I was starting to worry that you may have been right, how busy can she possibly be not to answer a single call or send a simple message? It has been two weeks since our date and I have not heard from her at all, not a peep. The suffering was starting to settle in, I was realizing that Heather was rejecting me, it was about to be another night of crying, punching the walls and screaming. But, just now I had an epiphany, just now everything has made sense and I am emailing to tell you how wrong you are.

Heather is not ignoring me, we had an amazing date and she truly loves me. We are meant to be together; it is obvious. So why has she not been answering my calls or texts? Well, the most logical conclusion is that she has lost or broken her phone. Of course! That is why she has not responded. It all makes sense. She probably really wants to speak to me but has no way of contacting me. She probably misses me so much, she is up right now in her bed thinking about me, wondering what I am doing. All week she has been stressing, worried that I have forgotten about her, but she cannot call me and she has no idea where I live. I feel so sorry that she has had to go through this. How many nights has she spent crying over me? Poor Heather. Why didn't I realise this sooner, I could have gone down to the coffee shop and seen her. Well I won't waste any more time. Tomorrow morning I am waking up and going straight down to the coffee shop. I know she works Saturday mornings. I will go in and she will be so delighted to see me, I bet she runs over to me and gives me a big hug and a kiss and tells me how much she missed me. It will be a magical moment. I can't wait.

I can't believe I doubted her love. That was your fault, you filled my head with those negative thoughts. Heather would never ignore me, she loves me with all her heart. And tomorrow, when we are hand in hand I will show you, I will prove you wrong and you will be apologising to me!

I have lost Heather and I don't know why. The reason I was getting up in the morning, the spring in my step and the smile on my face has been taken away from me. Everything I was so happy about, so grateful for, has now been ripped from my fragile fingers.

I went to the coffee shop this morning to see Heather. I was so excited. I got there at 8am, right when it was opening. I could see through the window the shop was empty, just Heather, as beautiful as ever, standing behind the counter. As I walked through the door Heather immediately looked up and saw me. I was waiting for the smile, I was waiting for her to jump over the counter and come to me, I was waiting for the hug, the kiss and the loving words. There was nothing there. As soon as Heather saw me she had an awkward nervous look on her face, she looked back down.

I stood there staring at her, wondering what was going on, she was putting every ounce of energy into not looking at me, she looked terrified. I walked over to the counter and carried on staring at her, I didn't say a word, I just waited. She had her head down, still trying

196

to avoid me. After about a minute she eventually acknowledged me.

"Can I help you?"

That's what she said, after everything, after our amazing date, after weeks of me trying to speak to her, that was her response to me.

"Heather, I have been trying to reach you for weeks now."

"I know."

"Oh, I thought you lost your phone."

"No I haven't."

"So you have been getting my messages?"

"All your messages and your calls. Honestly it was quite creepy how much you called me. You have been freaking me out. Please can you just leave me alone."

"I don't understand."

"Just leave me alone, you're basically stalking me and I feel nervous, I don't want you to call or text me anymore."

"But Heather please, I just want us to go out again. I want to take you to a restaurant."

"I don't want to go out with you again, I just want you to leave me alone, do not contact me."

"But... we had such an amazing time."

"Please just leave me alone."

"I love you Heather, you are my soul mate."

"Just leave me alone!"

She screamed. A man from the back came rushing out, it must have been the manager. Heather started crying.

"What's going on?" he shouted.

"Nothing I..."

"Mark, this man is harassing me, please tell him to leave." She was stuttering through a veil of tears.

"Alright mate, get out of here now before I call the police."

"I wasn't harassing her, I just..."

"Get out now! I'm dialling 999."

He pulled out his phone and started calling the police. He was furious, Heather was still crying. I don't understand what had happened, I don't understand how I caused all of this chaos, and I don't know why, but yet here I was standing in the middle of this turmoil that I was somehow responsible for. There was nothing left for me to do, I just ran, I ran and ran and ran.

I don't remember what happened after, the last few hours are a complete blur. I remember running, the next thing I remember is waking up in my bed. This could have all just been a bad dream, but I don't think it was, it all felt so real, that pain I felt was real, it was definitely real and it still hurts.

After I woke up I went into the bathroom to use the toilet. The bathtub was full, my mum must have had a bath earlier and forgot about it. I pulled the plug and I just stayed there watching the water drain, slowly, slowly, I watched that full tub descend into emptiness. The water that was once so warm and so desirable has now been discarded down the sewer, as though it never even existed. When the last drop disappeared down the drain I burst into tears. I couldn't control myself.

17th August 2022

Patient: Simon **[redacted]**

Session Number 17

Today was the biggest relapse in our therapy so far. The past two weeks have been a huge setback for Simon and unfortunately the coming weeks will need a lot of rebuilding. I was truly disappointed to read Simon's emails over the weekend, although I was expecting this outcome, it was still difficult to read how badly the situation with Heather affected him. It was clear that Simon had once again built up an image of greatness in his mind, and the realisation that this did not actually exist has sent him on a downwards spiral. I knew this session was going to be tough, but we have been here before so my plan was to go back to basics.

Simon arrived wearing a grey t-shirt with grey jeans and black loafers, the same outfit he would consistently wear in our early sessions. He looked tired, weak and pale; there were black bags under his eyes, his hair was very untidy and his patchy beard was starting to poke through. I believe he has been oversleeping once again and the lethargy has returned. Simon entered the room and immediately sat on the chair, his head was down and he was staring intensely at the floor.

I knew it was going to be a struggle to get Simon talking in this session, so I started off trying my best to get Simon to open up. I told him that I read through his emails and I was sad to hear what had happened. I asked how he had been feeling since the incident on Saturday. Simon did not respond, he just continued staring at the floor. I asked again and Simon still stayed quiet. I let the silence remain a little longer. Finally I pressed Simon further.

"Simon, what you went through on the weekend was sad, I know it was, but if you are going to overcome it we need to speak about it."

He looked up, a cold soulless expression and stared at me.

"There's nothing to speak about." A serious monotonous tone.

"Yes there is. I would like to know how you are feeling."

"Does it matter?"

"Of course it does."

"No it doesn't. It doesn't matter."

"Simon, it matters, that is why you are here, that is why you have been coming here all this time. Now, you had quite an emotional weekend, tell me how you are feeling."

"I am suffering."

"Ok and why are you suffering?" Simon did not answer. "Come on Simon, talk to me, tell me why you are suffering?" He remained silent. "Is it just about the situation with Heather, or is it more than that?" Still not a single word. "Simon I can't help you unless you talk to me, now please tell me, why are you suffering?

"Why does a triangle have three sides?"

I was slightly stunned by this response. I wasn't sure what he meant by this. I asked him to elaborate, but he just repeated himself.

"Why does a triangle have three sides?"

"I don't understand what you mean?"

"Why does a triangle have three sides?"

"Can you explain that for me?"

He buried his head into his hands and stayed there. Ten minutes had passed of complete silence; Simon remained in that afflicted position, not saying a word, not making a noise, I could barely hear him breathe. I really didn't want to just give up, I knew I would be deeply disappointed if I didn't get more out of him, I thought I would try one last time.

"Simon, I want you to know, everything will be ok. I know you have had a couple of hard weeks but we are going to get through this together. I am here, and don't forget how much we accomplished before. The reason we made such progress was because you shared with me, you spoke to me and together we managed to pull you back up. You have fallen again, there is no shame in that. Life is full of ups and downs, in fact we need to experience the downs in order to appreciate the ups. We need to feel sorrow and sadness, we need to sometimes suffer so we know how amazing happiness is, so we know how great fulfilment is. Do you understand?"

Simon looked up, he slightly leaned forward indicating he was paying attention.

"What you are going through now is actually a necessary thing. The horrible parts of life are necessary, they need to exist so the great parts of life can exist. Just like cold cannot exist without hot, like the tall cannot exist without small, happiness cannot exist without suffering. My job has been to help you create as many great parts of life as possible *and* to help you deal with the terrible parts, because unfortunately you cannot escape them, they are a part of life. At the moment you are down, but just like before we can work on bringing you back up, and when you do come back up you will be better for it. You will be stronger, more emotionally secure, your character will have developed more, you will be a better person. I just need you to try. So let's do this again, come on."

I was waiting for Simon to react, for him to seem enthused, for him to say something. Unfortunately I got nothing. Exactly what I feared, he turned his head and stared out the window with that blank expression on his face. He had checked out and there was nothing more I could do. Soon enough our time was up.

Before he left I set Simon a homework task and asked him to email me his current thoughts and to open up about his suffering. Simon didn't seem to take notice of my request, he got up and walked out. I am very concerned by his behaviour, it reminds me exactly of our first session almost 5 months ago. For us to be back here considering how far we had come is very troubling. I am hoping Simon will open up in his next email and I will be waiting eagerly for this to pop up in my inbox. This will hopefully put me in a better position next week to help him open up a bit more. Among the unfortunate incidents Simon has experienced these past few weeks with his friends, with the job interview and now with Heather, I strongly believe stopping the medication has greatly added to his downfall. I am almost afraid to keep raising this as the last time I tried Simon became very aggressive, but it is imperative that Simon starts the medication again. I will have to focus on this in our next session and hope that Simon has a better reaction.

It is conscious, It is awake, It listens, It is all knowing, It is all present and It controls everything. Everything is in Its reach; we all belong to It and It can do whatever It wants to us. We are all powerless. We pretend to be Gods because we are too insignificant to see. But now I can see, I have grown, and the more I grow the smaller I become.

It is talking to me now. Right now, as I type this email. These voices haven't gone away. Since our last session I started to hear whispers, throughout the day faint words in my ear. I had no idea what they were or where they were coming from, but they were definitely there. They would come and go, very quiet, but I could hear them. "Suffer", they would say. "You deserve everything you get". I would be lying on my bed and they would start. I would be having dinner and there they were. "You're vile, you're despicable," and on and on. My mother, frustrated and worried, insisted that there was nothing there, she was adamant, but she was wrong, I could hear them, they were there.

As the week went on the voices became more frequent and louder. "Feel this pain", would scream in my ear, "Suffer, suffer, SUFFER!" They wouldn't leave me alone. I would hold my head and cry, I would turn the TV up, put music on, just bang on the walls, anything to try to drown out the voices. But nothing worked, they weren't going away, every day they were getting stronger. The neighbours complained to my mum that I was being too loud. She came into my room and saw me crying, banging on the walls with my TV volume on max. When she saw me she started crying too, she ran and hugged me. "She hates you" "everyone hates you", "look at what a horrid creature you are".

I haven't slept properly in days, they will not let me sleep, they will not let me think, they will not let me relax, they will not let me be, they are constantly screaming at me.

Yesterday was the worst day. From the early hours of the morning I was woken up by these voices in my head. "Suffer" "your life is pain" "your world is agony" "you are scum" "you are atrocious" "you deserve everything" "you must suffer, suffer, SUFFER!" This was constant, not a moment of respite, not a moment of silence. I stayed in my bed all day, I didn't move. I stayed there listening to these voices over and over and over and over. I was waiting for them to stop, for just one second, just so I could hear something else. But they wouldn't stop, they just kept on, getting louder and louder and louder. By the evening they were shouting;

multiple voices, all shouting all at once. It was unbearable. I couldn't take it anymore. I got out of bed and I just screamed, as loud as I could, as long as I could. I screamed until my throat hurt, until there was no breath in my lungs. The longer I screamed the longer I could go without hearing these voices. I screamed and screamed and screamed. My mum burst into my room with the most terrified look on her face. As soon as I saw her I ran for the door, I pushed her out of the way and ran downstairs out of house. I could hear her shouting for me but I carried on running, I don't even know how long I was running for, I sort of left myself for a bit.

When I gained self-awareness I had no idea where I was, I couldn't recognise anything, nothing made sense, I had never seen this area before. There were no houses, there were no roads, it didn't look like anyone had ever been here before, it was just a muddy field as far as the eye could see, nothing but weeds, nettles, dead flowers and a thick fog that strangled everything ahead. There were hundreds of bare trees standing, and loads of dead trees lying on the floor, one of the trees was bleeding, it was still alive but dying slowly, I approached it to see if I could help, but it brushed me away with one of its branches, it wanted to die alone.

I started walking, I didn't know where to go I just knew I had to get out of this place. It was very dark, I was struggling to see. Up above there was nothing but dark clouds, you could feel the sorrow emanating from them. The temperature dropped, I hugged myself to try and stay warm. As I walked I could hear crunching beneath my feet. I looked closer to see what I was standing on, I realised it was thousands of dead butterflies, they were everywhere, covering the entire ground. I couldn't move without crushing their poor dead bodies, it was horrible, it made me sick.

I was feeling cold, lost and scared, I was shivering and I didn't know what to do or where to go. Suddenly I thought I saw a figure in the distance. As I approached I could see it was definitely a person. In a delighted panic I started running over praying this person could help me. As I approached I was utterly perplexed by what I saw, the closer I got the clearer the figure became, I couldn't believe my eyes until it was undeniable but there she was, out of all the places at all the times Heather was here, right when I needed her. My guardian angel was here to rescue me. I called out to her, she turned, she saw me and smiled. Such a beautiful smile. I ran to her. As I got close her face changed, she started looking furious; as I got even closer I reached out to her, she looked away, turned her back and started running from me. I continued to run after her but the more I ran the further she got from me. I was screaming for her, pleading with her to just stop, to talk to me, to help me get out of this cold dark place. I needed her, but she refused to stop, she carried on running, faster and faster until she was out of my sight, gone, she left me here, in this cold dark place, she left me lost, she left me to die.

As I carried on wandering through the darkness, crushing the lifeless bodies of thousands of butterflies I got a glimpse of a light far off into the distance. I started walking towards it. As I approached I could see it was a house, a single Tudor house out in this deserted wasteland. I was desperate, I hoped there would be someone inside who could help me find my way. I reached the house, all the lights were on, so I knocked on the door, there was no answer. I knocked again and there was no answer. I started banging furiously on the door asking if anyone was there, telling them that I was in urgent need of help, but no one answered. I went round the back of the house, there was a big window looking into a living room. Once again I was shocked at who was there - Colin, Thomas, Andrew and Antonio, all sat on comfortable couches, drinking beer, talking and laughing. There was a TV on the wall with football playing, and a dining table with three large pizzas. They all looked so happy, so relaxed, they were having a great time. I know I was upset with them but it was such a relief to see them, here at my lowest ever point, they were all together and they could take me in. I knocked on the window but no one responded. I started banging as hard as I could but none of them even noticed, it was like they couldn't hear me. I started punching the window as hard as I could, my knuckles split open, there was blood smeared across the glass, but still, none of them responded, they didn't even look across to see me. I started screaming, I started crying, I was begging them to notice me, begging them to let me in, begging them to let me join them, I wanted to be part of that warm house, I wanted to sit down, I wanted to eat and drink, to laugh and smile. It was cold outside and it was so lonely. Eventually I saw Thomas get up, very casually he walked over to the window. I was hoping that he finally heard me. As Tom approached the window I saw him tug on a string and immediately the blinds came falling down. I then heard all the boys start laughing. I was shut out. They didn't want me, there was no place for me there.

I carried on walking, I didn't know where to go, but I just felt like I had to carry on. Some time passed, I can't tell you how long, and still I was lost. I tried to make some sense of where I was, hoping I could find some route back to normal, but everything looked the same. Then, ahead of me in the distance I noticed a floating see-through cube hovering about 20 feet above the ground with what appeared to be a man standing inside. I ran up to the cube, as I got closer I could see clearer and it definitely was a man standing inside. He was still, very quiet, a lifeless figure just standing there staring into the sky.

"Excuse me, excuse me!" I shouted. The man slowly looked down at me. He looked very peculiar, he had no discernible facial of features, almost like a three-dimensional shadow.

"Yes" he replied. I was relieved, this person was alive and he noticed me. Now I was just hoping he could help me.

"I'm lost."

"Of course you are." He replied.

"I'm not sure how I got here."

"Most people aren't sure how they end up here, that's for sure, but here you are."

"What is this place?"

"This is the Cedar Forest."

"Cedar Forest?" The man slowly nodded. "Do you know how I can get out of here?"

"You want to get out?"

"Yes."

The man laughed.

"Oh no, there's no getting out of here. When you're this far down, you never leave."

"Far down where?"

"That you should know."

"Please, I really need to get back home, I'm tired, I'm in pain, I'm alone, I just want to get back."

"That's why you're here. Is that not clear?" I shook my head in confusion. "You've been down here before, but you spent too much time, so now this is where you belong."

"I don't understand what you are saying."

"You stared too long Simon. There's nothing you can do now. You should have learnt to look away."

"How do you know my name?"

The man pointed, I turned around and standing behind me was massive billboard sign.

Simon **[redacted]**
Application Unsuccessful.

I turned back to the man in the cube.

"Please, there's got to be a way out." I screamed.

"Things are not the way you want them, things are the way they are. You cannot accept them, so you here is where you are."

Within a second the cube shot into the sky and disappeared from my site. Once again I was alone, there was no one or nothing else around. I didn't know what to do, so I just carried on walking. I don't know how long I was walking for, 1 hour, 5 hours, 10 hours I have no idea. It remained dark, it remained cold, it remained empty, just an endless muddy land, with naked trees, chopped trees and now millions of dead butterflies beneath my feet. I was so tired, I was in so much pain, I tried to carry on, I didn't want to stay in this darkness forever, I had to get somewhere but no matter how much I walked I couldn't seem to get out of this horrible place. Eventually my legs gave way, I collapsed to the muddy floor. I stayed there, lying on my back. I was lying there probably for hours, I could feel myself slowly sinking into the mud. I thought that if I stayed lying down long enough then eventually this place will swallow me up. I didn't want to die here, but I had no energy to carry on. As I lay there staring at the sky sinking deeper and deeper I could see a sheet of paper slowly float down and land on my chest. I picked it up...

Simon's Journal
Fill me up

That was it, the rest was blank. I held the paper close to my chest for a little while, I then felt the urge to carry on moving, but I was so tried and weak. Still, I tried. I had a sudden rush of energy, I put everything I had into pushing myself up, I manage to get unstuck from the mud and I managed to push myself up onto my knees. I was however terrified by what was waiting for me. As I elevated my torso, there sitting in front of me was my father's grave. I don't know why it was there but somehow it was there. I tried one last time to stand, I hobbled back onto my feet but then I stumbled again, holding onto the tombstone as support. I started crying hysterically, I started screaming, the melancholy had settled. At that moment it suddenly got very windy, all the dead butterflies started blowing away. The ground started shaking, I could hear roaring thunder. The sky opened, the clouds parted to reveal a canvas of millions of stars and planets spinning in a violent and deranged frenzy. The thunder got louder the wind got stronger. It was the Universe Linda, It was talking to me. I could feel It. Finally after all this time, It revealed Itself to me. After all these years of complete silence, the Universe finally confronted me, It spoke to me Linda, It proved to me that It is alive, It thinks, It feels, It desires, It acts, and It is angry with me. I have been so wrong and I am ashamed. I have denied the existence of reality. I could feel the anger filling up the atmosphere around me. The Universe was telling me that It wanted me to suffer, that It was putting me through all of this on purpose. It was silent all these years to torture me, but now It has made Itself known, It has made Its feelings known. The Universe hates me. I was crushed by this realisation, but I knew it was true, everything I have gone through, my entire life, it is not down to chance, it has not been random, I am detested, I am abhorred by the reality that created me.

My whole body was injected with angst and despair, I felt so heavy, so much pressure being forced on me, as I leaned on my father's tombstone it couldn't bear the weight, it smashed into a thousand pieces. I fell back down to the floor.

I don't know what happened after, I can't remember. I gained awareness and realised I was lying on my bed; I could hear my mother outside my room crying. I immediately started writing this email because I don't want to forget anything that happened. The voices are still screaming at me, but now I know what they are, It is the Universe, It is talking to me, It is reminding me how much It loathes me, and how much It wants me to suffer.

24th August 2022

Patient: Simon **[redacted]**

Session Number 18

Today was the most troubling session I have conducted with Simon and I am truly worried for his wellbeing. I was extremely concerned when reading his latest email yesterday morning. If I was to take Simon's email as a genuine account of his experience of the week then Simon is undergoing severe audio and visual hallucinations, delusions and extreme paranoia. This cognitive breakdown is most likely down to a combination of the unfortunate recent events in his personal life combined with the sudden stopping of his medication. From what was conveyed in his journal log, it showed Simon to be in the worst mental state yet and I did not know what to expect today, I was very anxious and nervous about the session. Initially I thought it could be possible that Simon was having a bad episode and used the journal as an outlet for some creative writing to help cope with the situation he was in, unfortunately this was not the case.

Simon arrived 25 minutes late, this is first time he has ever been late for a session. He was wearing the grey t-shirt, grey jeans and black loafers, however his clothes were covered in mud, dried mud all over his t-shirt, smeared across jeans and completely covering his shoes. I could even see dried mud on his face, hair and hands. His hands were also bloodied and bruised, there was dried blood all over them and all his knuckles had cuts and scabs. Simon's eyes were very bloodshot, he looked like he had not slept all week. His hair was very messy, the patchy beard was back and he had very strong body odour.

He sat on the chair, he was shaking his feet and arms. He stared at me, dead in the eyes. I was expecting him to be staring at the floor trying to avoid eye contact, but he was looking at me, he wouldn't break focus, he stared intensely right at me, whilst continuing to shake and fidget.

"Simon" I began "what happened to you yesterday?"

"I told you. Didn't I?"

"Why are you covered in mud?"

"When I was lying on the ground in that dark forest, I told you, didn't I?"

"Was this before the universe spoke to you."

"Yes, yes, yes, the universe Linda, it spoke to me, finally, it spoke to me."

"I see."

"You know, don't you?"

"Know what?"

"You were there."

"Where?"

"At the dark forest, you sent me that note didn't you? Simon's journal. That was you, you tried to get me up so the forest wouldn't swallow me. You tried to help me. That was you wasn't it? Wasn't it?"

I paused; Simon believed everything that he had explained in the email. The fact that his hands were bloodied and his clothes were dirty meant that he definitely was somewhere the past few days, but he was also having very lucid hallucinations.

"Thank you Linda" he continued. "You always did try to help me, even though it was all in vain, you tried, you're the only one who tried. I appreciate you looking out for me at the forest."

"Why has it been all in vain?"

"Like I told you, the universe hates me."

"How do you know this Simon?"

"It told me, it has been telling me all week. I told you, didn't I?"

"Yes you did, but how do you know it was the universe?"

"Oh it was, it has been whispering to me all week, it revealed itself to me in the forest, it revealed its hatred for me, right after you sent me that note. I wished you had stuck around to see it. It was so powerful, so angry. And it hates me so much."

Simon started laughing, hysterically.

"Why are you laughing Simon?"

"It is talking to me now."

"The universe?"

"Yes, it is talking to me, right now. It is telling me that I am boring you, that you can't wait for this session to be over. That you are fed up with me."

"Listen to me Simon, what you are hearing is not real. These are hallucinations, this is not the universe talking to you. You are not well, ok. Please understand, these voices you are hearing are not real."

"Your voice or the universe's?"

"The universe's."

"How can you say that Linda. The universe is very real. It is everywhere, it is everything, all we see, hear and feel. It is controlling us. I told you this, we spoke yesterday, didn't we?"

"Is it controlling you right now?"

"Of course. It is controlling me, and you and everyone and everything else. From the very start of time it has a plan for everyone. Everything you do, everything you choose, all your actions, desires, thoughts, feelings, everything, it has planned for you, it has created for you. You are following a set path that was put into motion the moment that time began. You are nothing more than a tiny cell in an infinite body that has been programmed to act in a specific way. We do not make our own meaning, we cannot create our purpose, this has already been put in place. This is all a grand design, a well oil machine, and all of us are a specific component, nut, bolt or screw needed for this this reality to exist."

"What does the universe want from you?"

Simon dropped his head. "To suffer."

"And why does it want you to suffer?"

Simon did not respond. He stayed in that position, sitting with his head dropped down. After a few minutes I asked again.

"Simon, why does the universe want you to suffer?"

"I don't know."

Simon started crying. Tear drops were falling on his mud stained jeans.

"I don't know why, but it hates me, the universe just wants me to suffer and there's nothing I can do to change this."

I let Simon cry it out for a while. He stopped eventually and looked up.

"No use in crying over spilled milk."

"It's ok Simon you can cry." Simon paused suddenly. His eyes widened as he stared at me.

"Linda? When did you get here?"

"Simon, you're in my office."

He looked around, panic stricken and confused.

"Right, right, it is our session isn't it."

"Yes"

"What were we talking about?"

"You were telling me about the universe, that it is speaking to you."

"Yes the universe, it spoke to me Linda, finally after all these years, It finally broke the silence."

"Simon, is the universe still speaking to you now." He nodded. "What is it saying?"

"It is telling me to leave. That I am wasting your time. That there is nothing I can change."

"Why can't I hear the universe Simon?"

"Because it is not talking to you."

"But why are most people unable to hear the universe. Why is it only talking to you? Do you not think if we are all part of the universe it would speak to everyone and not just one person?"

Simon shrugged. I tried my best to explain to Simon that what he was hearing were just hallucinations, that the universe is not speaking to him, this was his mind playing a trick. I tried to remind him of the joy he has experienced, that he created his own pleasure, his own meaning, and he done this through his own free choices; his life has not just been suffering. I tried my absolute best. Unfortunately I do not think one word landed, I do not think he took notice of anything I said. I finished speaking and he was just staring at me, his big red bloodshot eyes, completely empty.

Simon eventually got up.

"Thank you Linda. It is only when you try to leave you realise the door is locked."

He turned around and left the session.

I will be seeking additional professional assistance for Simon's sessions as I feel his condition and symptoms have greatly worsened in the last few weeks. This last session confirmed that Simon is having very vivid hallucinations, paranoia, false beliefs, delusions as well as confused and muddled thoughts. I am truly disappointed in how this particular course has gone, from what appeared to be a huge success and great improvement I now see Simon in the worst possible state of mind. Personally and professionally I feel devastated with this development.

31st August 2022

Patient: Simon **[redacted]**

Session Number 19

Session missed:

Simon did not turn up to his session today. The secretary called twice and there was no answer. I did not receive a journal log from Simon this week either. After our last session I am very concerned by the lack of communication. I will personally continue to call, if only just to make sure he is ok.

From: Linda@**[redacted]**
Sent: 01/09/2022 - 09:30
To: Simon@**[redacted]**
Subject: RE: Simon's Journal

Hello Simon

I am emailing you as I have not been able to reach you on the phone and I want to make sure you are ok. You missed our last session and you have not called or emailed to let me know why. The secretary tried to call you and left you a voicemail but you did not return the call. I have also tried a number of times to reach you and I have not been able to get through.

Please can you reply to this email just letting me know that you are ok? If you want to see me face to face my office is open, just let me know when you would like to come in and I will make time.

I would really appreciate if you could respond as soon as possible as I am getting worried. Thank you.

Linda **[redacted]**
Clinical Therapist

Tel: **[redacted]**
Email: **[redacted]**
Mob: **[redacted]**

I am Simon. For the first time I am here. I have tried to silence me, to ignore me, to bury me. But now I can no longer be denied. The truth has been revealed, this is the real Simon.

The last few weeks have not been a coincidence, what I have gone through has not been by chance. The Universe saw what I was doing, It was there in our sessions, It was there when I was with my friends, when I was speaking to Heather, when I was applying for my job. It was all around me, watching, waiting. Every move I made, every choice I made, every thought I had, It was there, monitoring me, making sure I stuck to the path. I tried to deviate from the path, these past 5 months, I have been trying to break free from the grips of the Universe. I wasn't even aware I was doing it, but that doesn't matter, I was doing it, I was going against a finely tuned organism. I was rejecting an absolute truth; I was a living breathing walking contradiction. I was doing what I was not supposed to, I was a mistake, and like a mistake, I needed correcting.

Everything has been planned for us, we each have our own purpose, we are all here for a reason and all of us collectively make up reality as a whole. We all have our part to play, no matter how big or small, we are all needed. Most people are set on their course and they just go with it, they don't stop and question, they accept reality for what it is, they accept their part in the grand design without even knowing they have accepted it. As long as we stick to what we are meant to do the Universe does not care, It will stay silent, stick to your path, remain in your lane - that's it.

Unfortunately this is not the case for everyone. Some of us will stop and question, some of us will wonder, this is when the Universe starts paying attention to us. And when we stop what we are meant to do, when we leave our path, when we reject our purpose, this is when the Universe breaks Its silence, this is when the Universe becomes angry, and this is when the Universe tries to fix the abnormality. I am an abnormality. This is me, this is the real me.

The Universe saw what I was doing. I was trying to create my own purpose, trying to forge my own meaning, trying to be happy and fulfilled. This was not what I was meant to be doing, this is not how life is supposed to be for me. The Universe needed to act. It waited patiently, It waited until I was getting comfortable, until I had started to succeed, It waited until I had built up some momentum, some pride, some joy, and then with one devastating swoop It destroyed everything in front of my very eyes. It demolished everything I built, It took it all away from me, leaving me nothing but suffering in the desolation.

On the outside people may see this as just bad luck, but that is wrong. There is no bad luck or good luck, there is nothing other than what the Universe wills. And the destruction of my life was the Universe rectifying an irregularity. Many will say that we cannot fathom the mysteries of the Universe, but light is given to those in misery, and the Universe revealed Itself to me. It had to remind me who I was so I never try to deviate from the path again. But why! Why were these terrors marshalled against me? What had I done, to the Universe that sees everything, why has It made me Its target? I have no peace, no quietness, I have no rest, but only turmoil, and all I want to know is why? From the Universe that shaped me and made me, why? And it was here that my questions were answered, here is where my purpose was finally unveiled. Here is where I discovered why I am here. Finally, the ultimate truth was laid before me, the revelation had arrived.

My purpose *is* to suffer, my purpose *is* to be miserable, to live with constant pain, anguish and anxiety. My role in this Universe is to be tormented, I have been created like this in order for happiness and pleasure to exist. It all makes sense. Without cold we cannot have hot, without tall we cannot have small, without near we cannot have far, and without suffering we cannot have happiness. The Universe wants me to suffer, It needs me to suffer, misery must exist, and I am its manifestation. I must be unhappy; people need to be able to see sorrow and grief and realise what happiness and joy really are. I am the horrible life that exists so others can appreciate their own life. I am the torment so the pleasure exists, I am the depression so the joy can exist, I am anxiety so confidence can exist, I am empty so the fulfilled can exist, I am lonely so the content can exist, I am grief so the satisfied can exist. I am despair, so you can smile. I am Simon.

That is it, all my life searching, waiting, believing. There it is, the ultimate truth. I have been created to live a life of pain and agony, that is my purpose, that is the reason I am here.

Everything is clear now, everything makes sense. I despise my own life and I know what I need to do. The Universe thought It corrected this mistake, but It didn't. I will not continue on this path, I will not do as the Universe wants. No! I will revolt! I will show It. I will deviate from the course. I will rescue myself from the clutches of the ruthless. I will not be forced into a life of suffering. I will not give the Universe what It wants. I am fighting back, I am rebelling, I am the anomaly that cannot be fixed; I am Simon.

Metropolitan Police Report

Case Number: 0119580
Date: 03/09/2022

Reporting Constable
Name: **[redacted]**
Collar Number: **[redacted]**

Reporting Sergeant:
Name: **[redacted]**
Collar Number: **[redacted]**

At 17:30 on 2ⁿᵈ September I was dispatched to **[redacted]** in reference to a reported suicide. I arrived on the scene at 17:50, paramedics were already onsite. A young man was pronounced dead at the scene, he had lacerations on both wrists. Death is suspected to be down to exsanguination, although we are awaiting an official post-mortem report. A blood stained knife was found next to the body, this has been sent down to forensics.

Onsite I was met with Officer **[redacted]**, we spoke with the deceased's mother, Janine **[redacted]**. The deceased is named Simon **[redacted]**. Janine had come home from work; after calling for Simon a number of times and getting no response she then went upstairs into Simon's bedroom to see if he was ok. That is when she discovered his body. She called emergency services straight away.

Janine explained that Simon had been suffering from severe depression and was undergoing therapy and medication. The last few weeks she had noticed a major deterioration in her son's mental health.

There seemed to be no damage to the property, no signs of struggle or forced entry. Neighbours have confirmed that they did not hear any disturbances throughout the day. We have confirmation that Janine had been at work all day.

We await the final post-mortem report however for now we are not treating this death as suspicious as it appears to be a case of suicide.

Printed in Great Britain
by Amazon